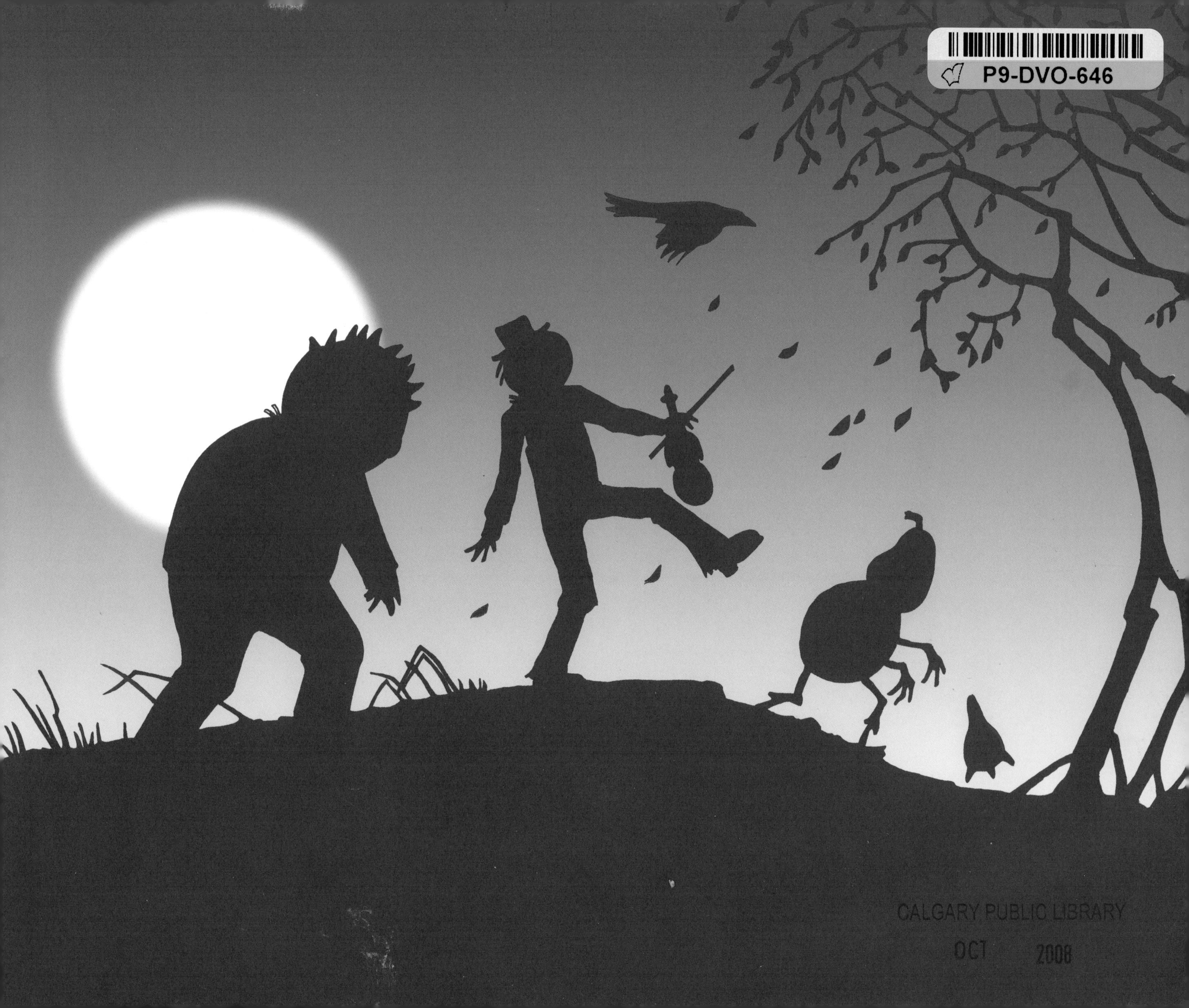

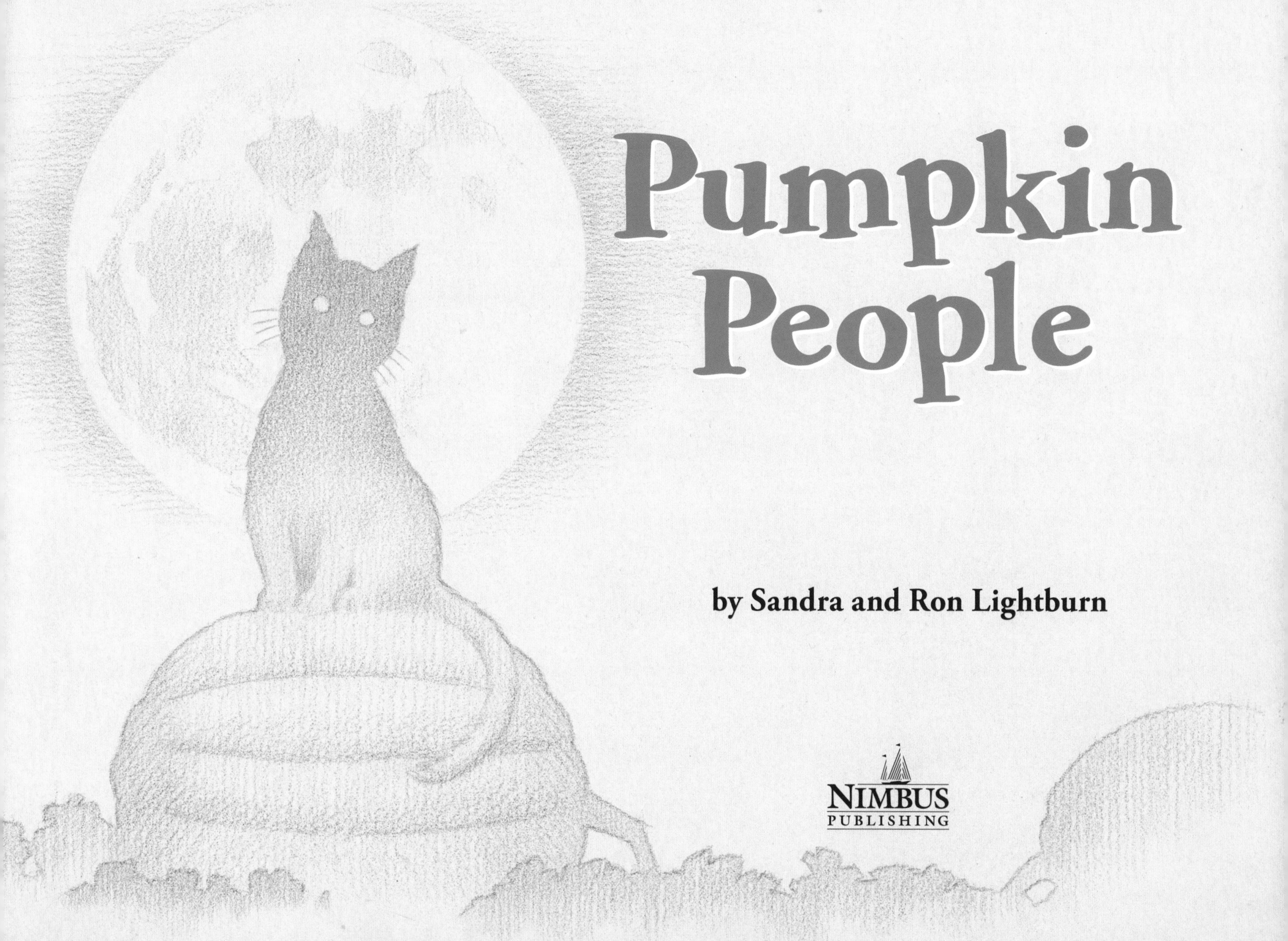

Pumpkin People

by Sandra and Ron Lightburn

NIMBUS
PUBLISHING

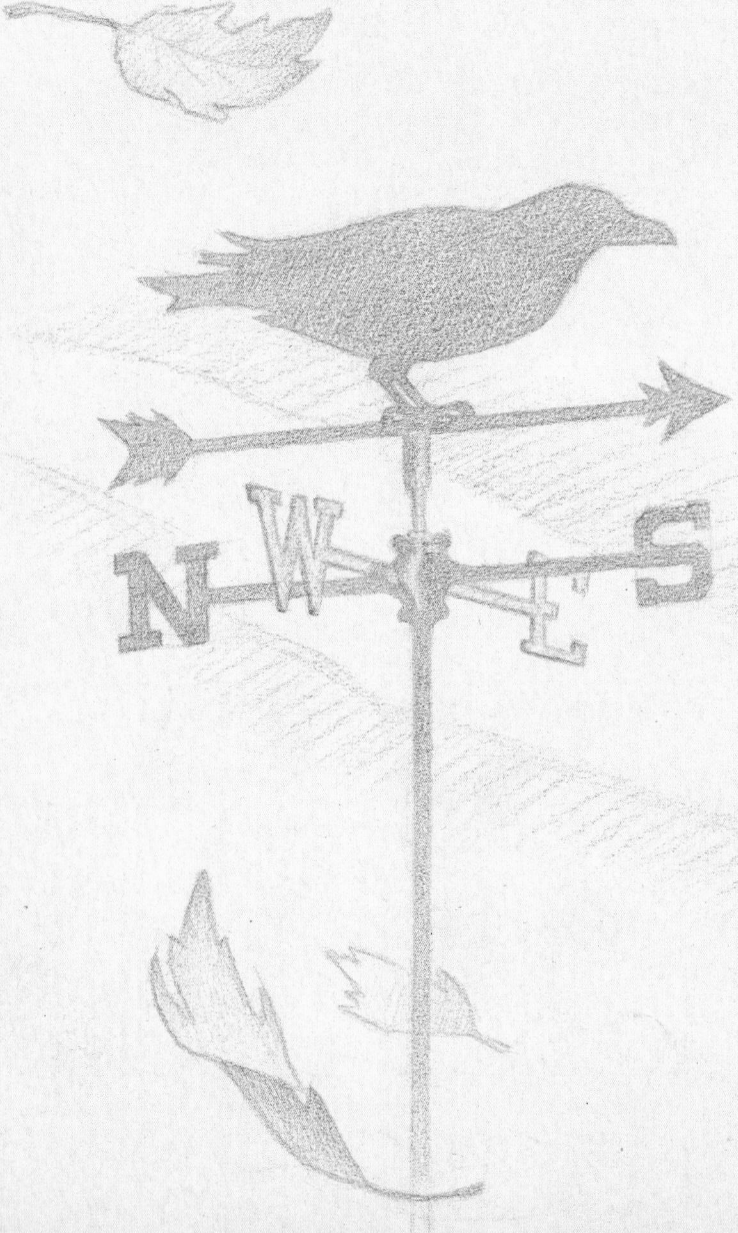
N
W
E
S

When summer's gone a change is seen.
The leaves have all turned half past green.

The air is cool, the nights grow long.
The wind will sing a mournful song.

An autumn moon hangs low and near
and pumpkin people time is here.

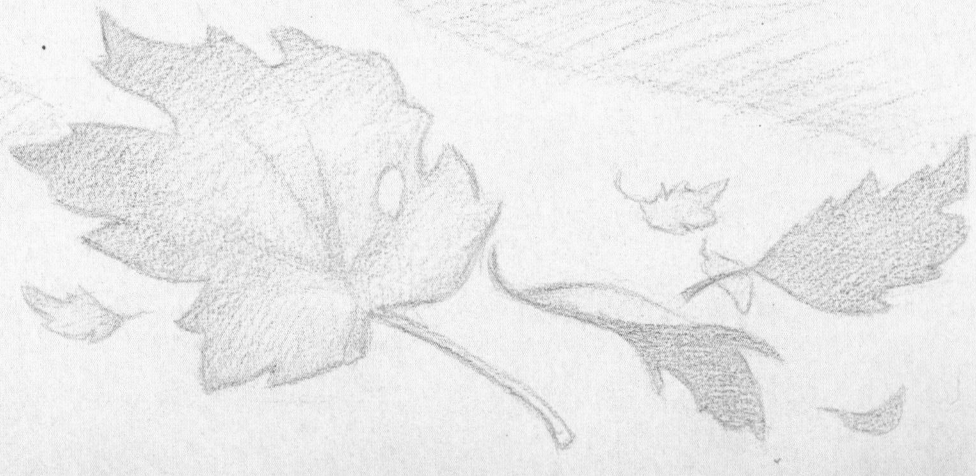

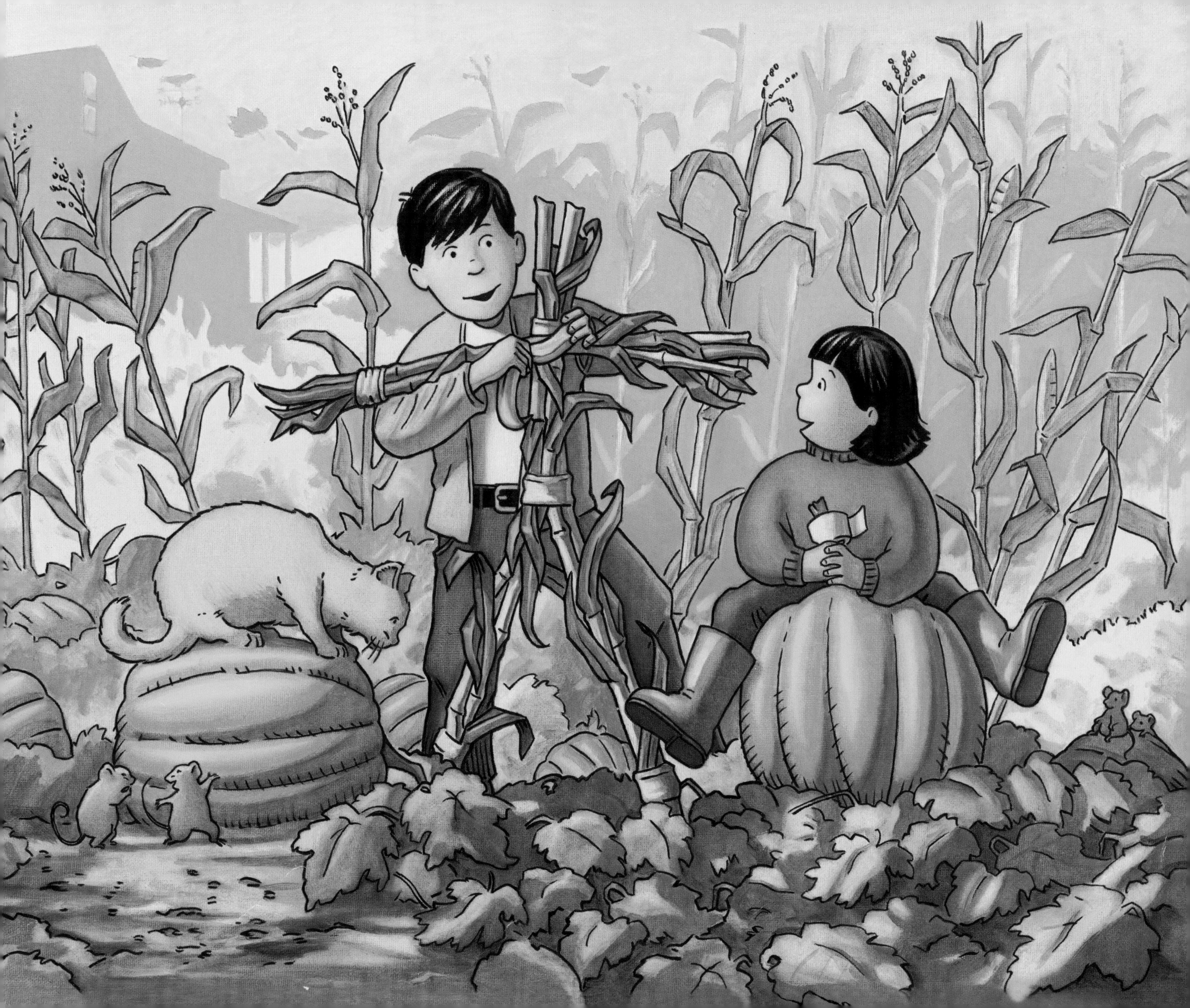

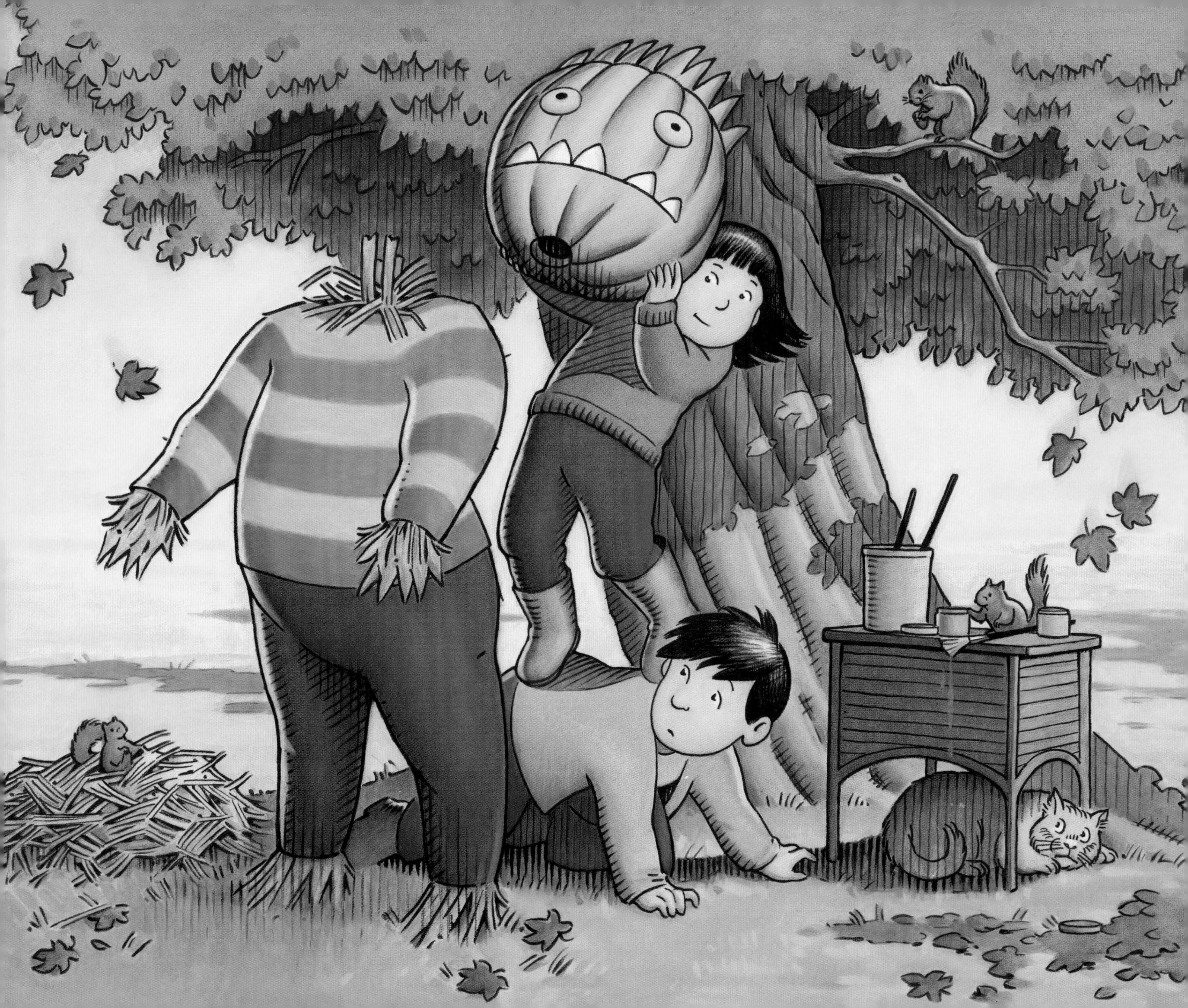

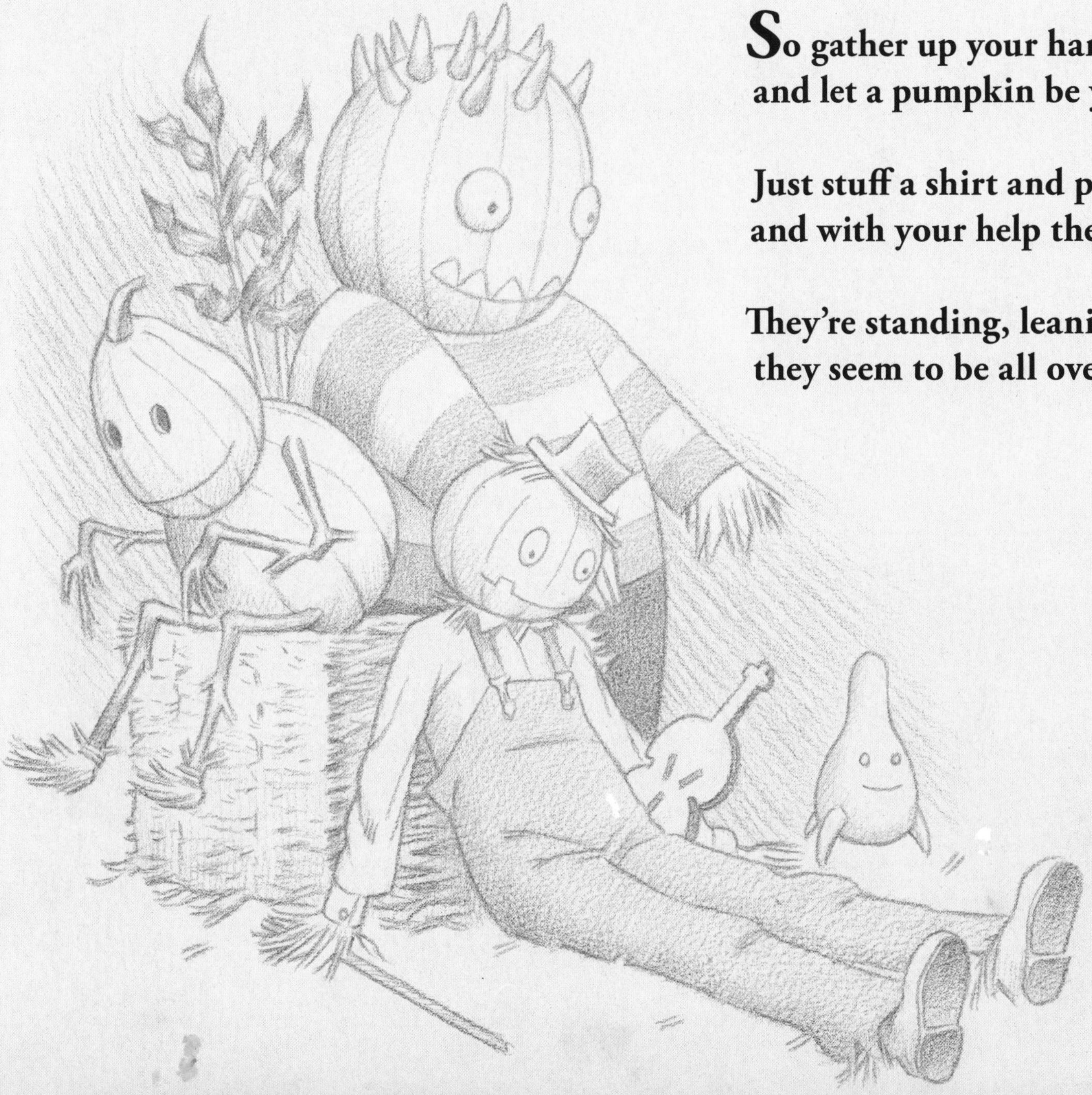

So gather up your harvest best
and let a pumpkin be your guest.

Just stuff a shirt and paint a face
and with your help they'll take their place.

They're standing, leaning, sitting down,
they seem to be all over town.

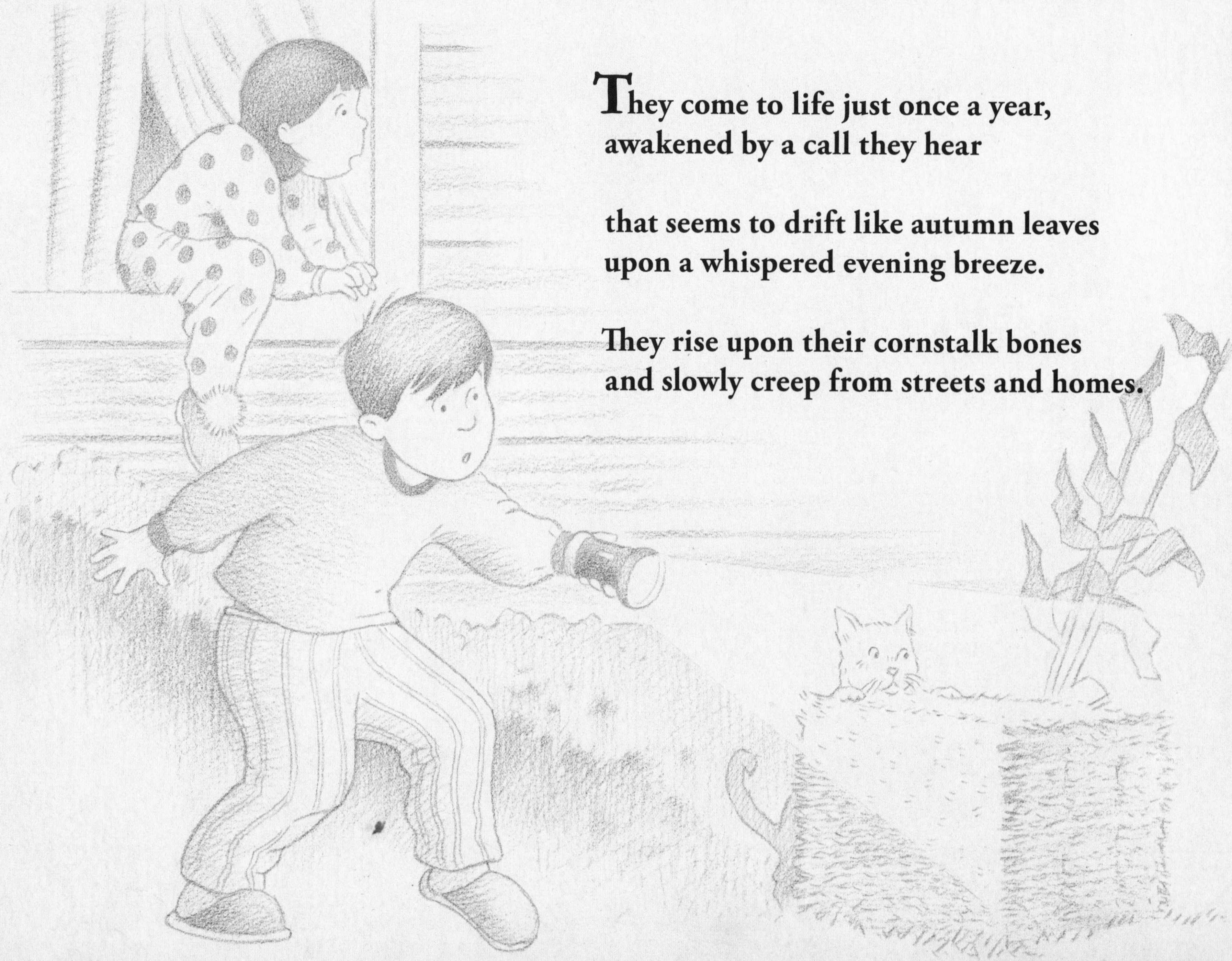

They come to life just once a year,
awakened by a call they hear

that seems to drift like autumn leaves
upon a whispered evening breeze.

They rise upon their cornstalk bones
and slowly creep from streets and homes.

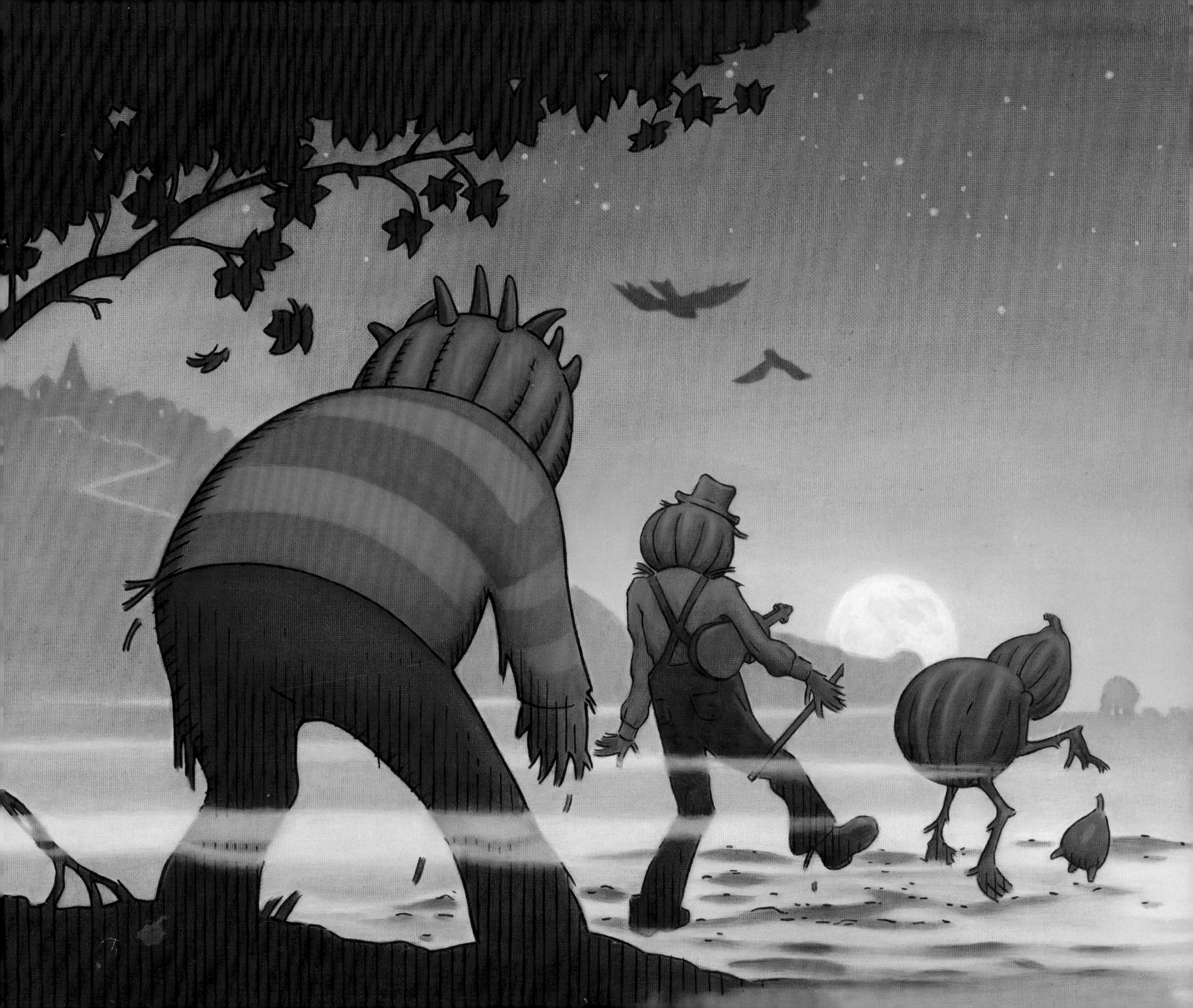

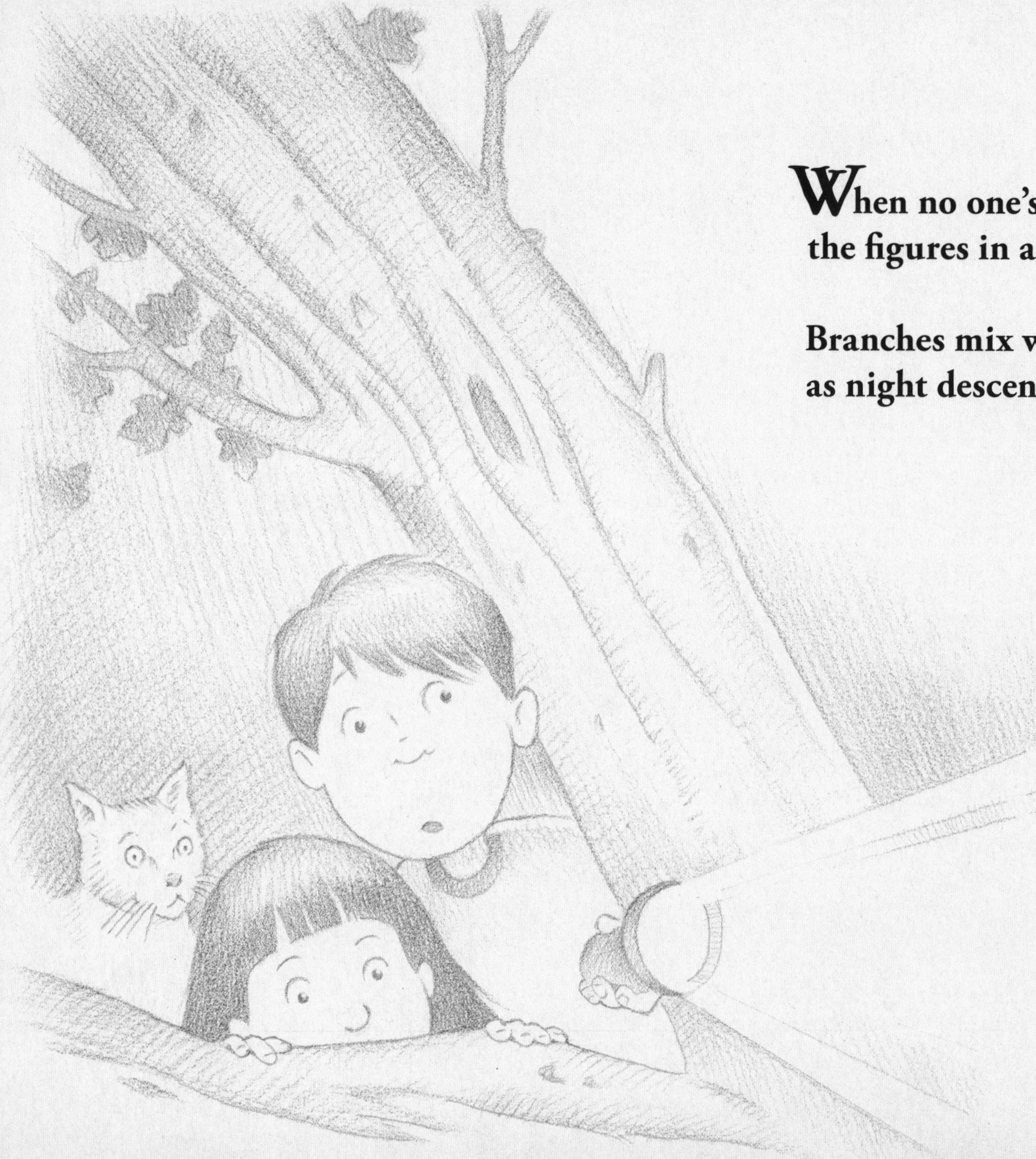

When no one's looking, no one sees
the figures in amongst the trees.

Branches mix with cornstalk limbs
as night descends and twilight dims.

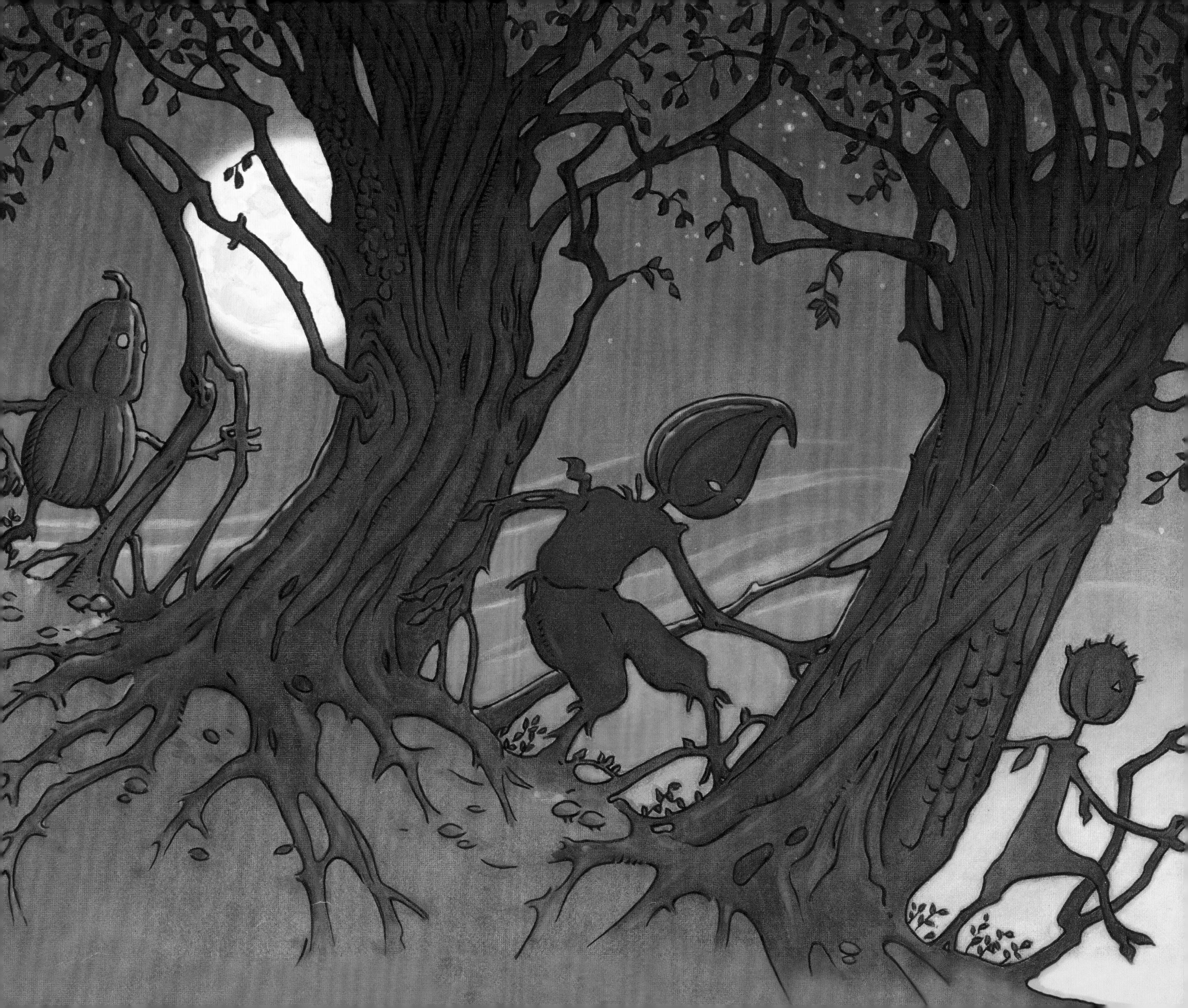

In fields they gather secretly
to celebrate so gleefully

the harvest of those autumn days
in odd and eerie pumpkin ways.

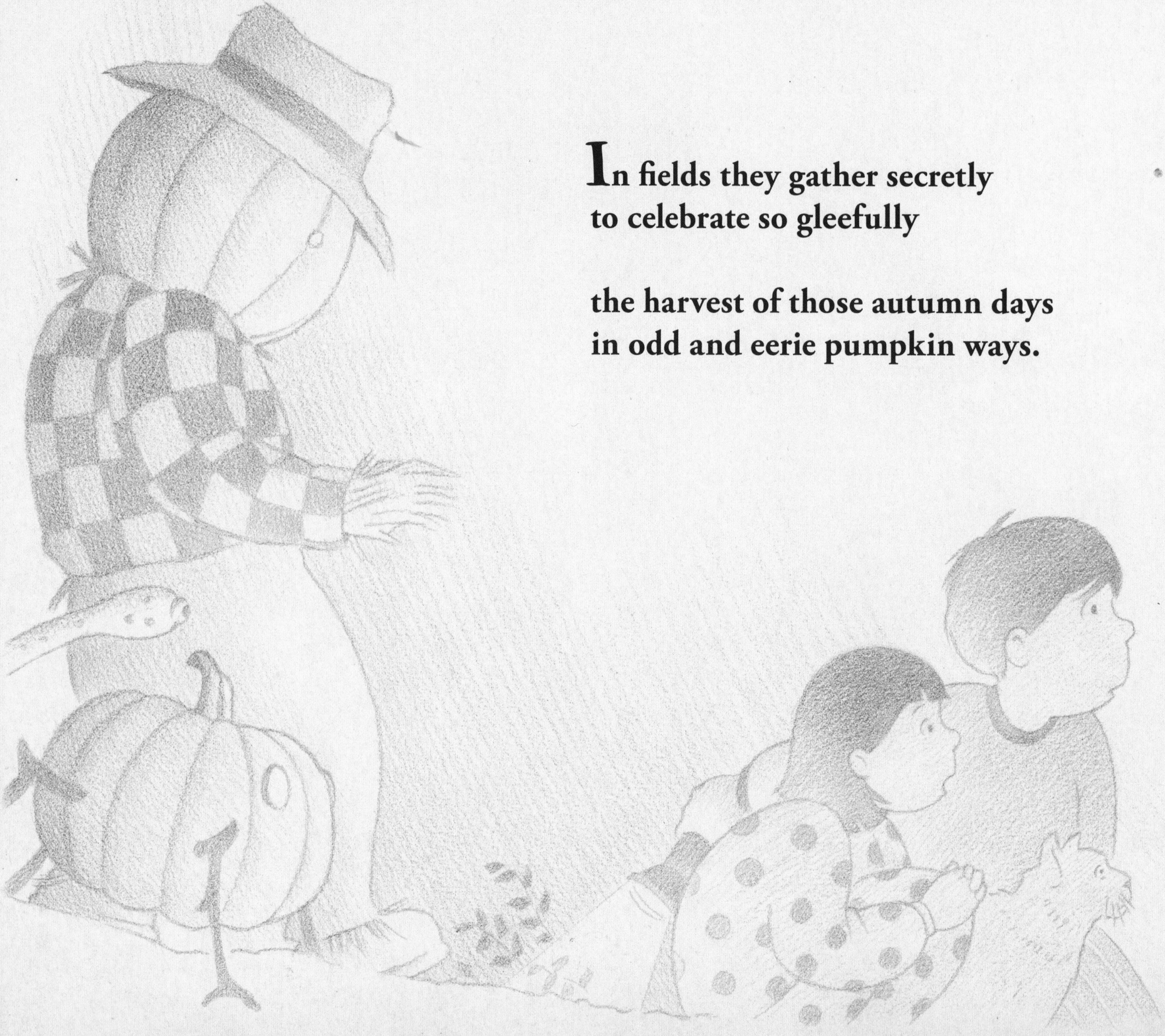

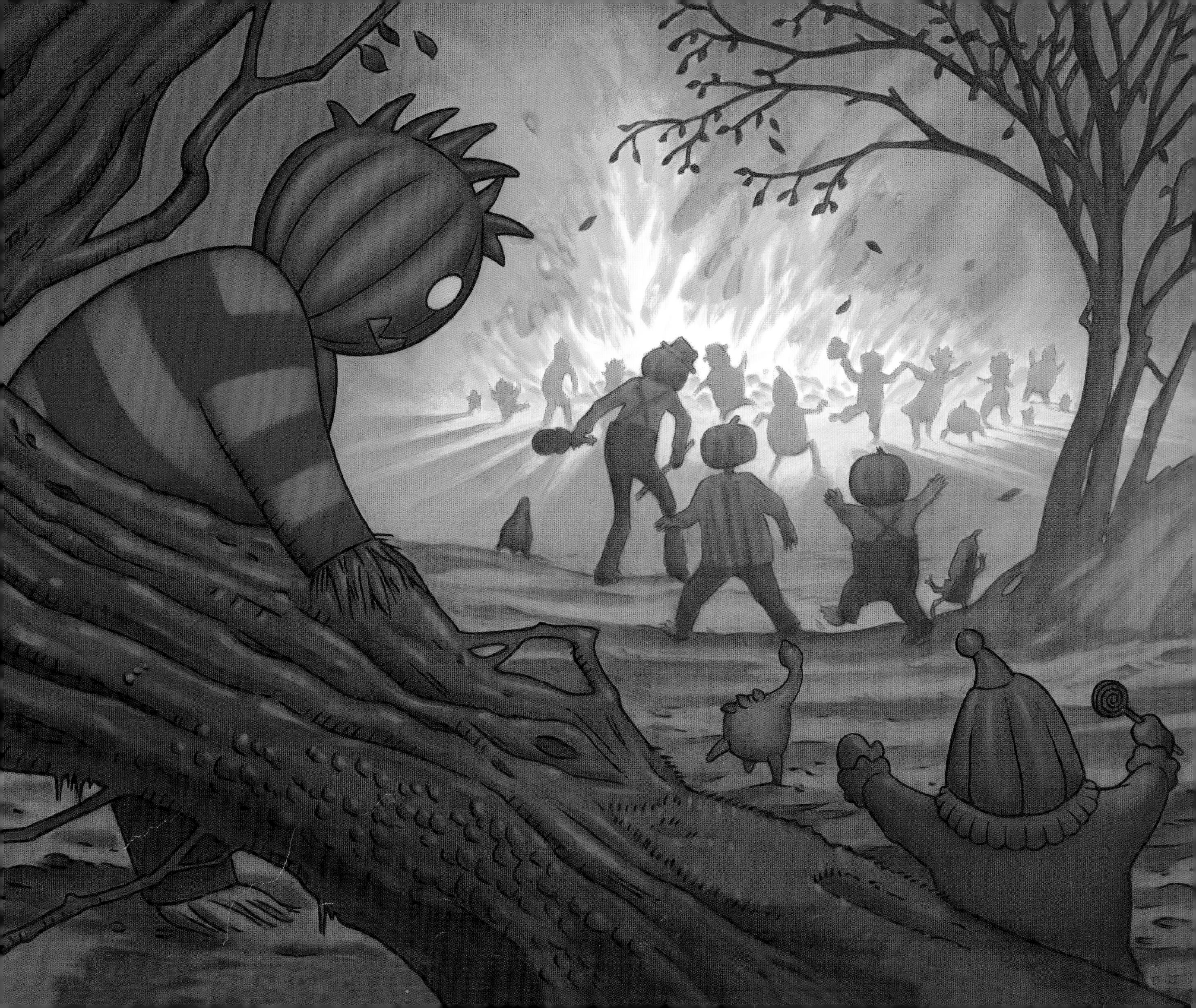

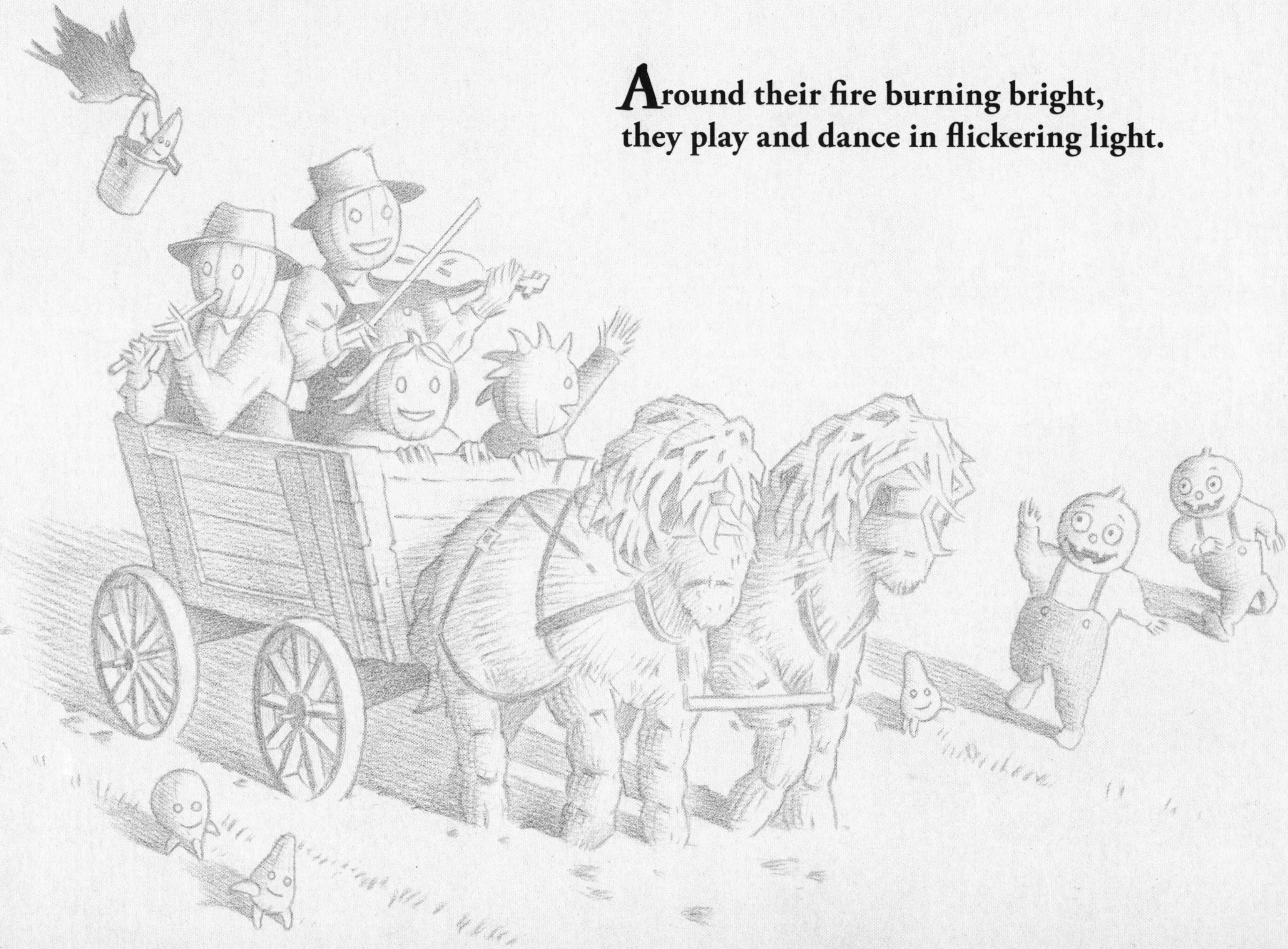

Around their fire burning bright,
they play and dance in flickering light.

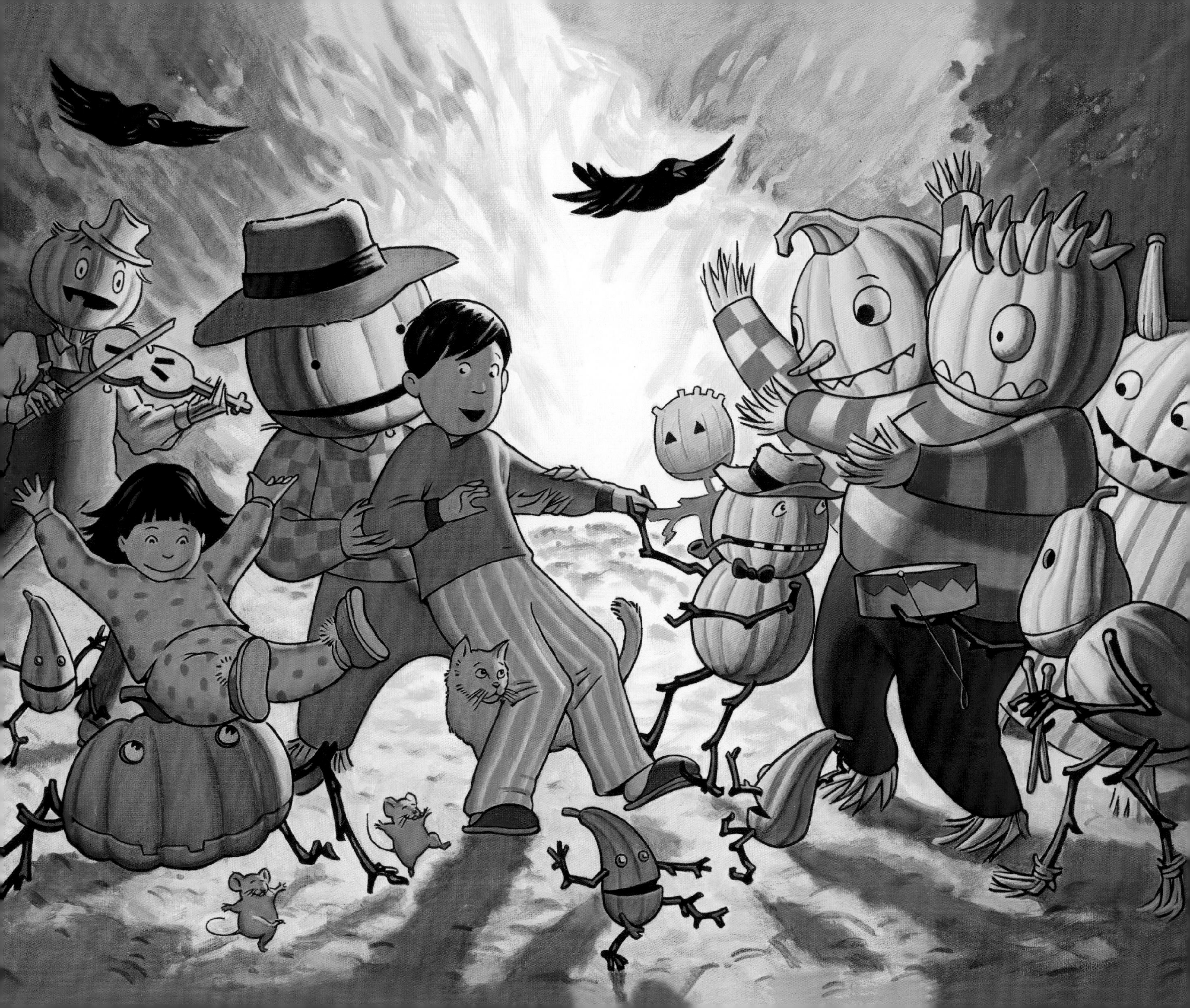

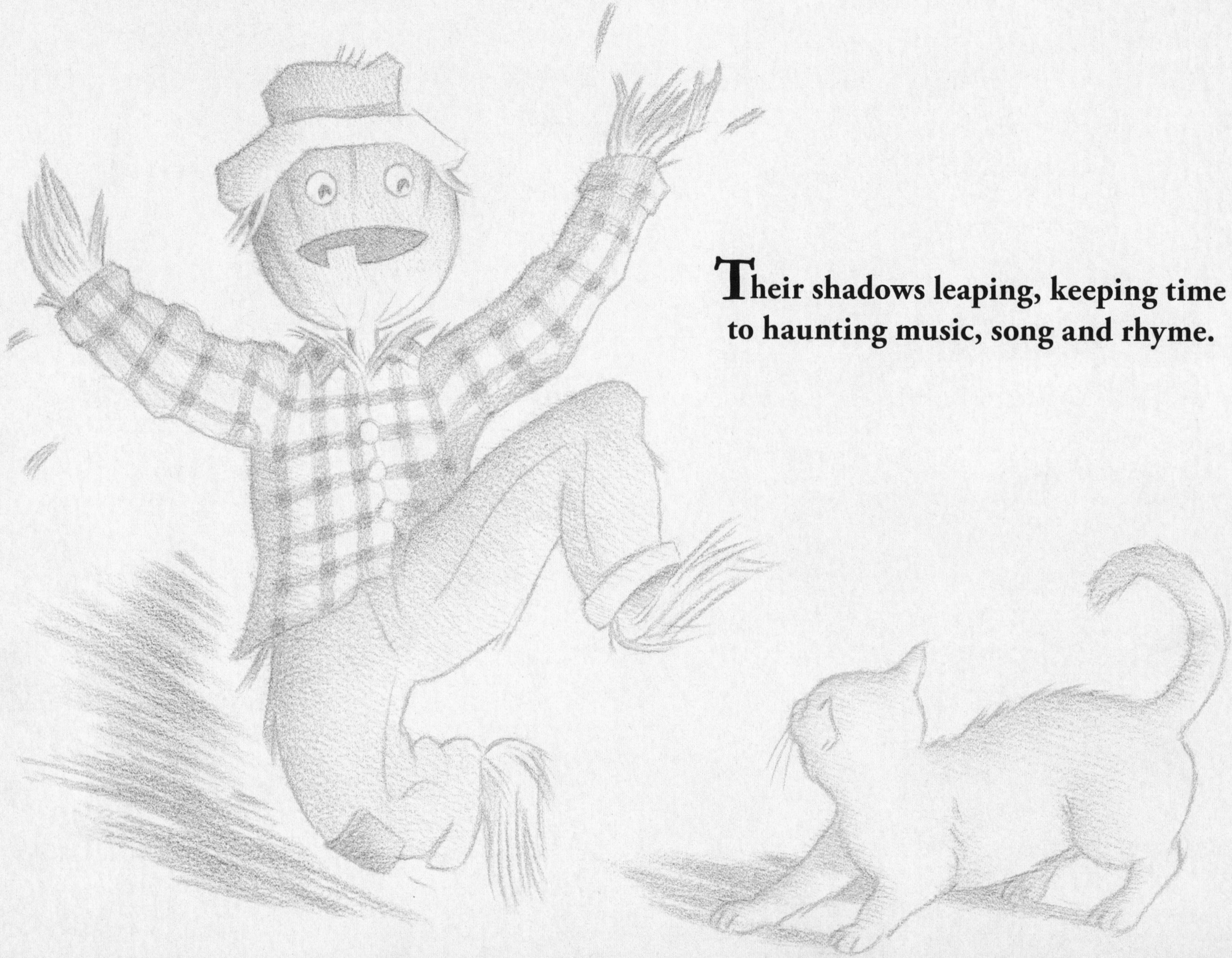

Their shadows leaping, keeping time
to haunting music, song and rhyme.

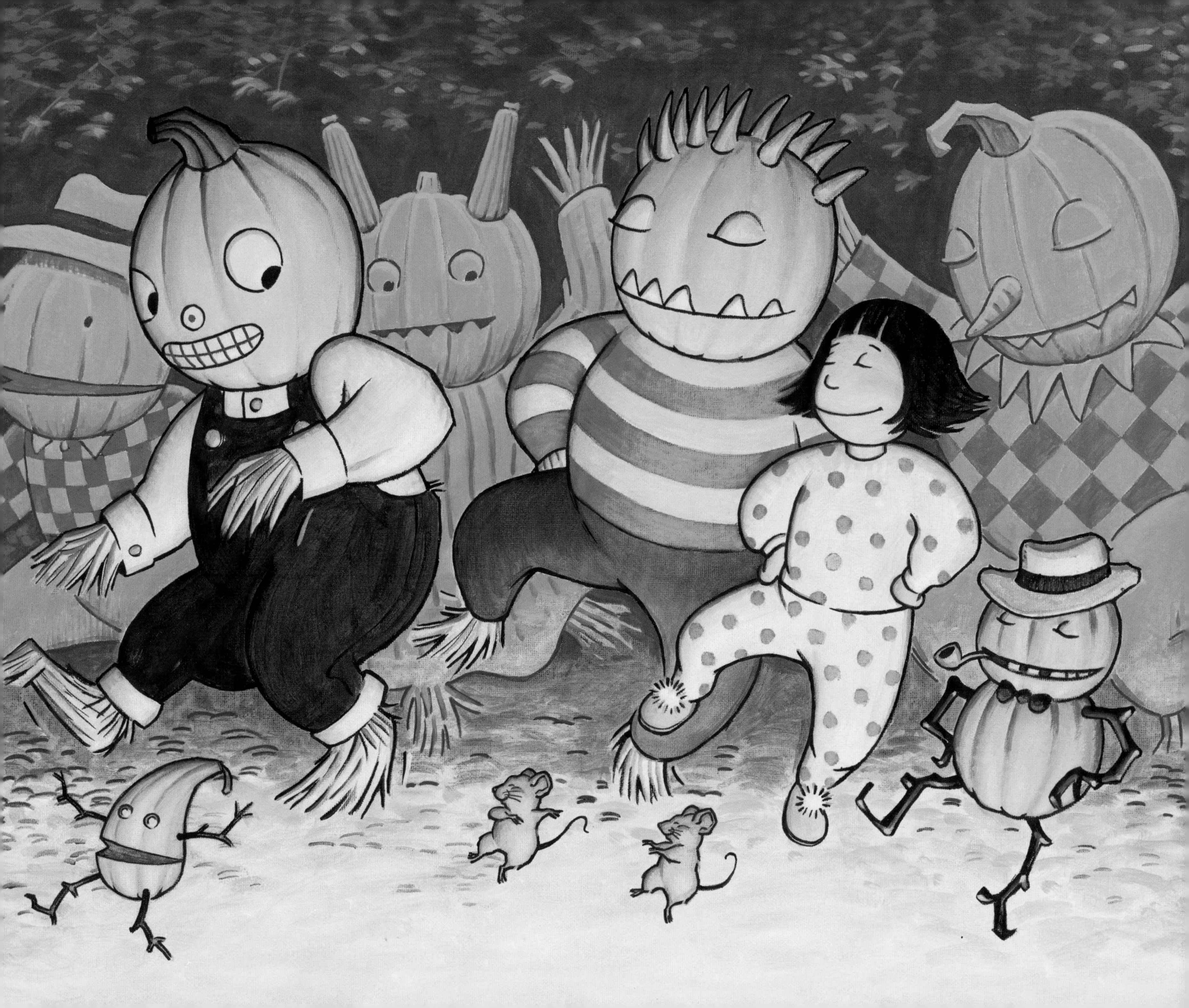

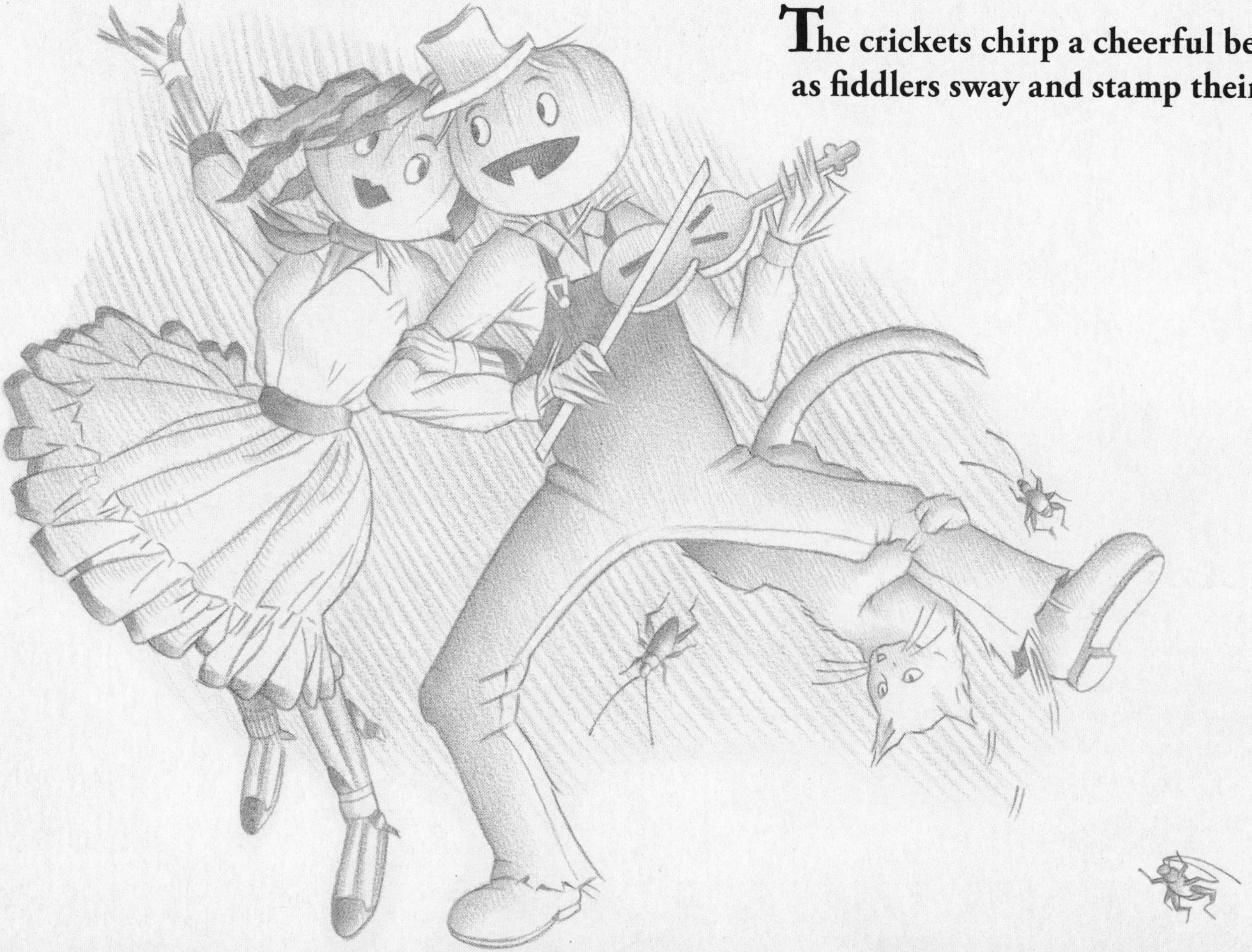

The crickets chirp a cheerful beat
as fiddlers sway and stamp their feet

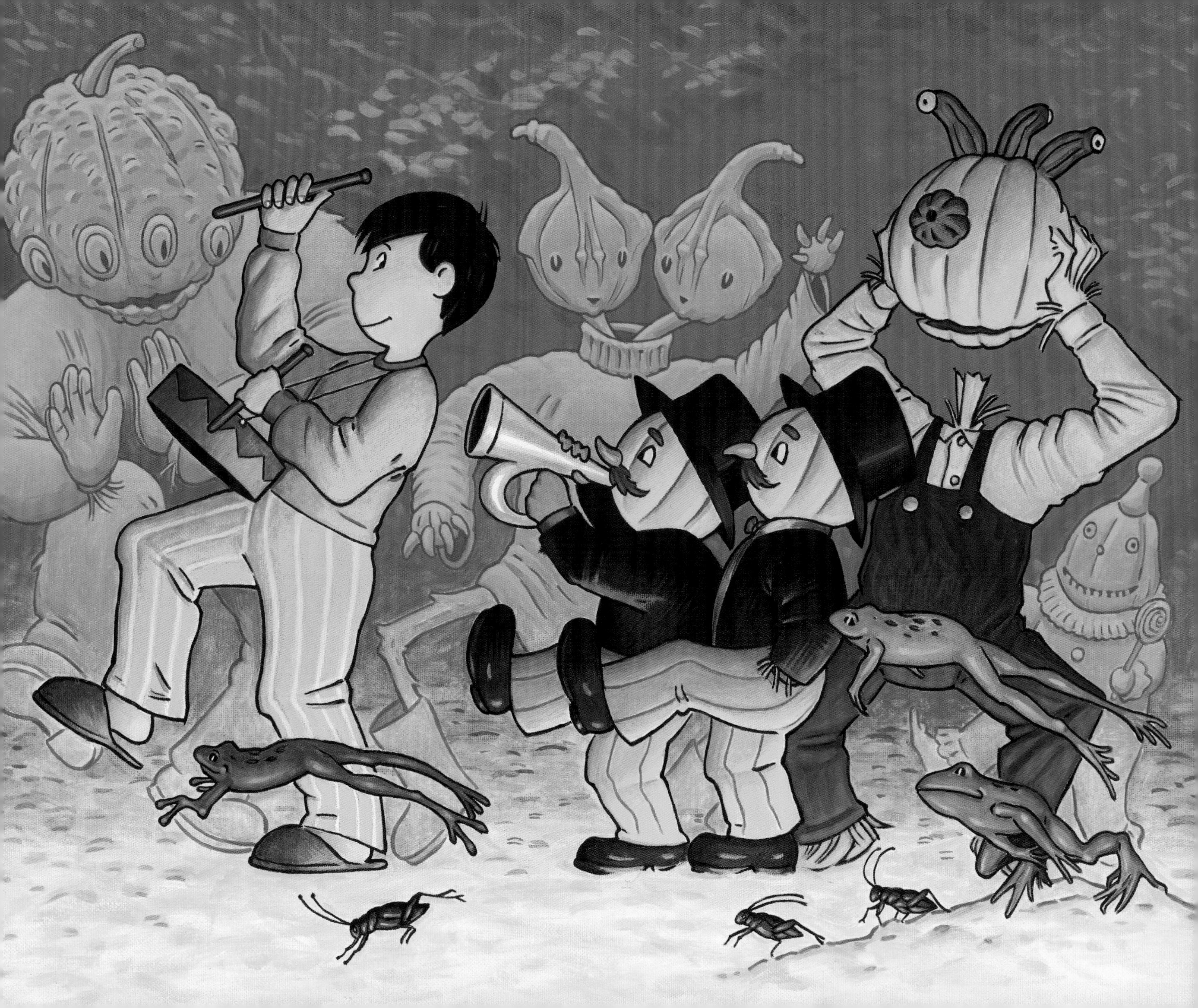

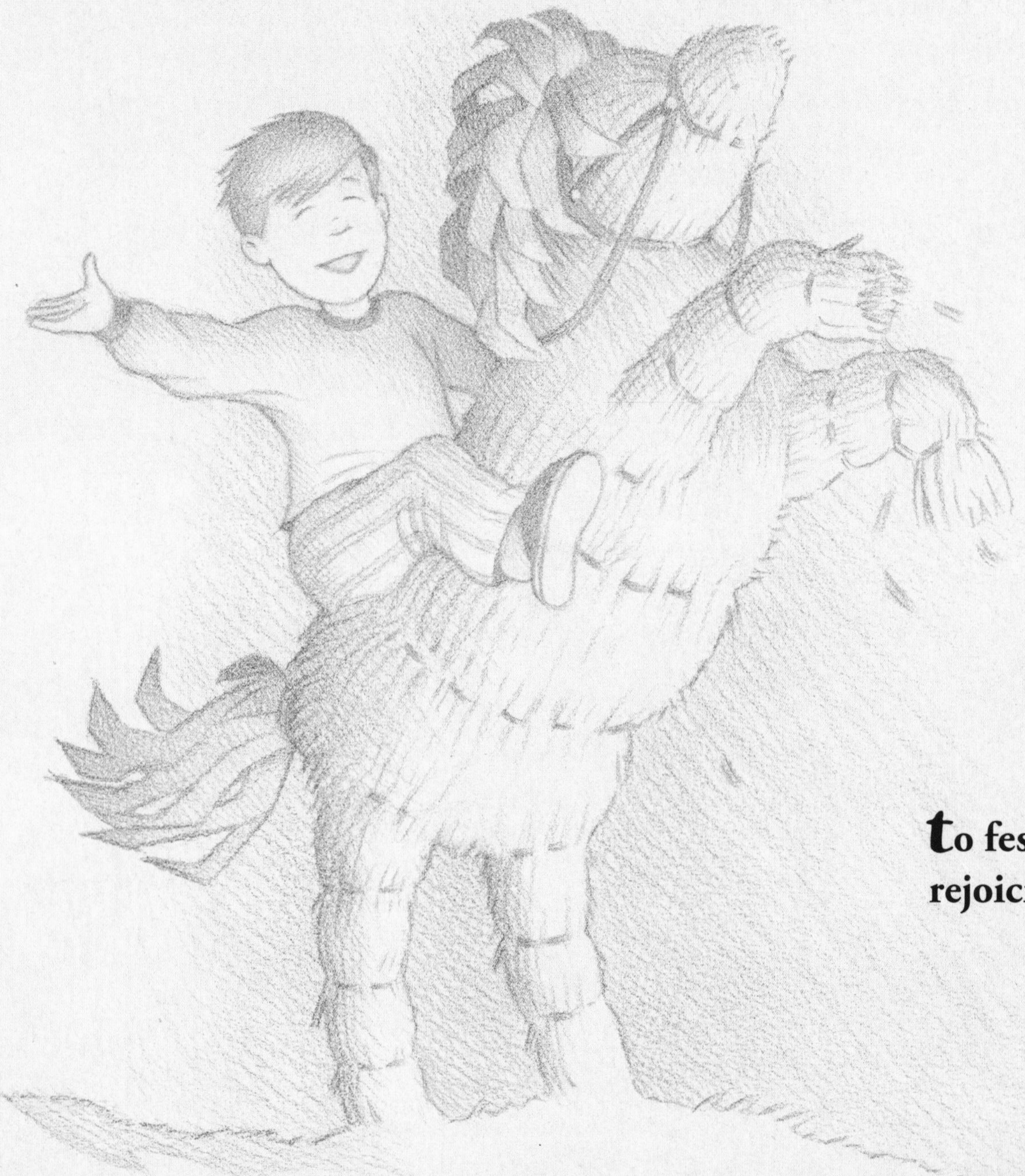

to festive melodies and chants,
rejoicing in their moonlight dance.

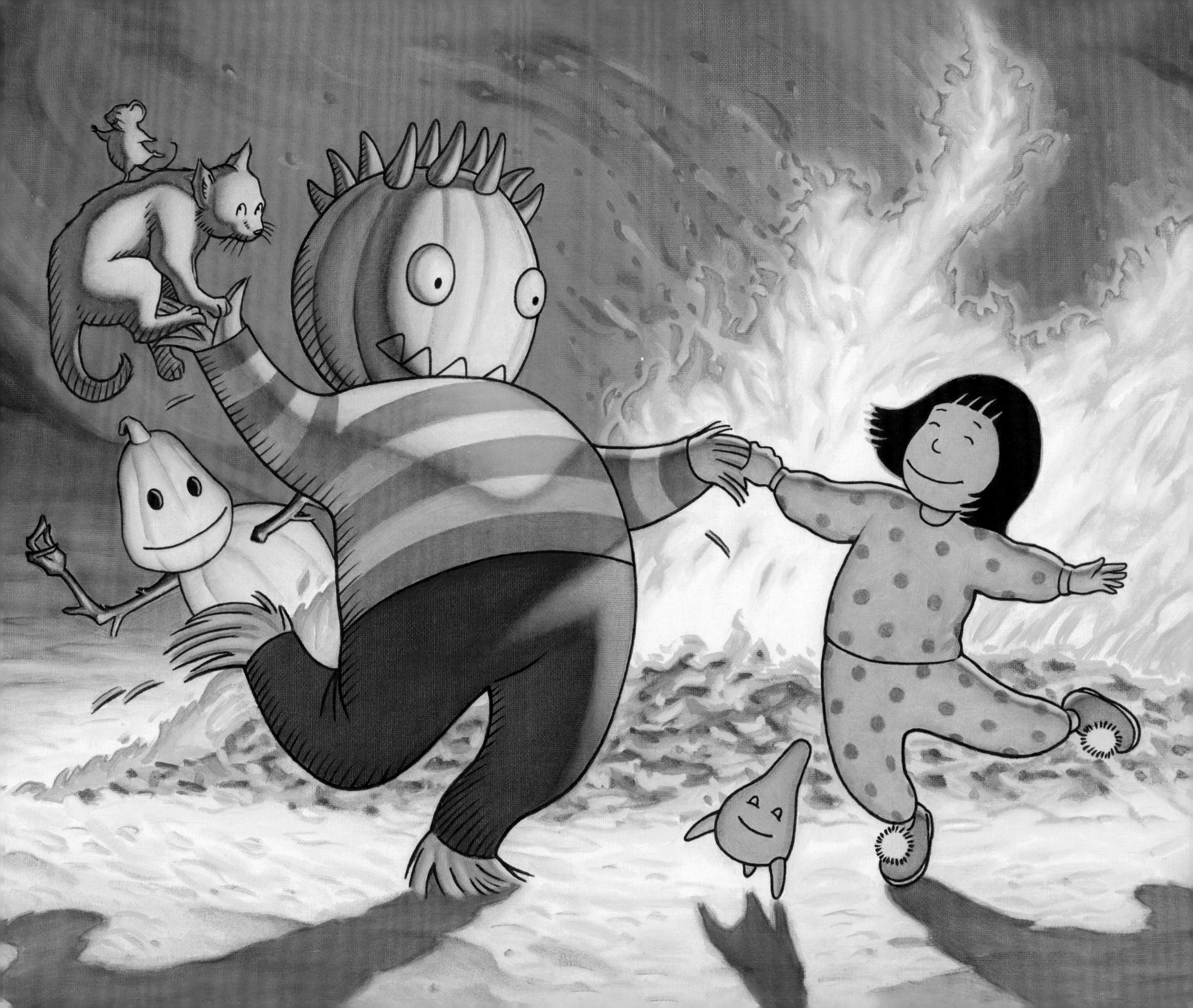

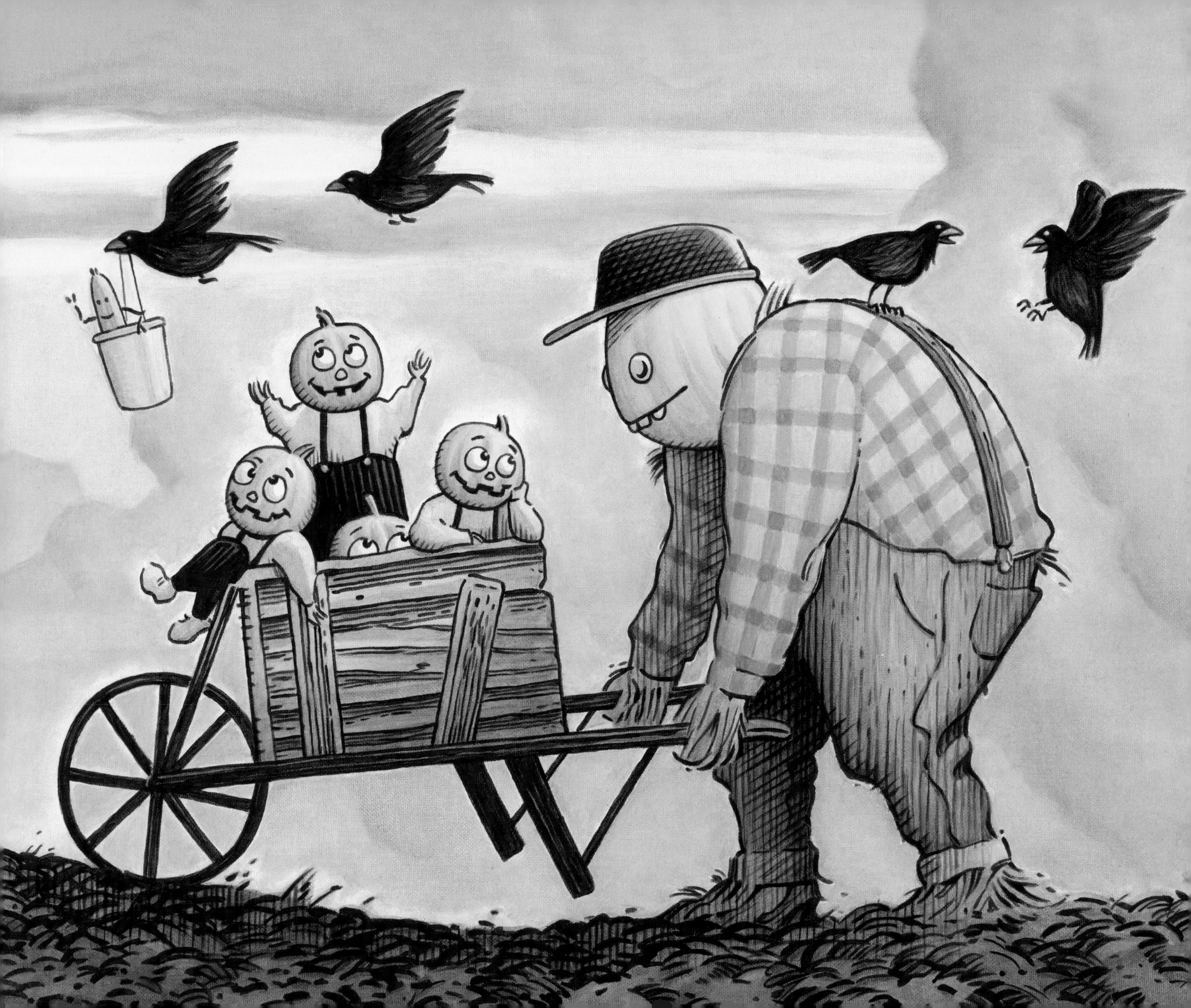

The gourds and squash join in the fun,
till dawn arrives and night is done.

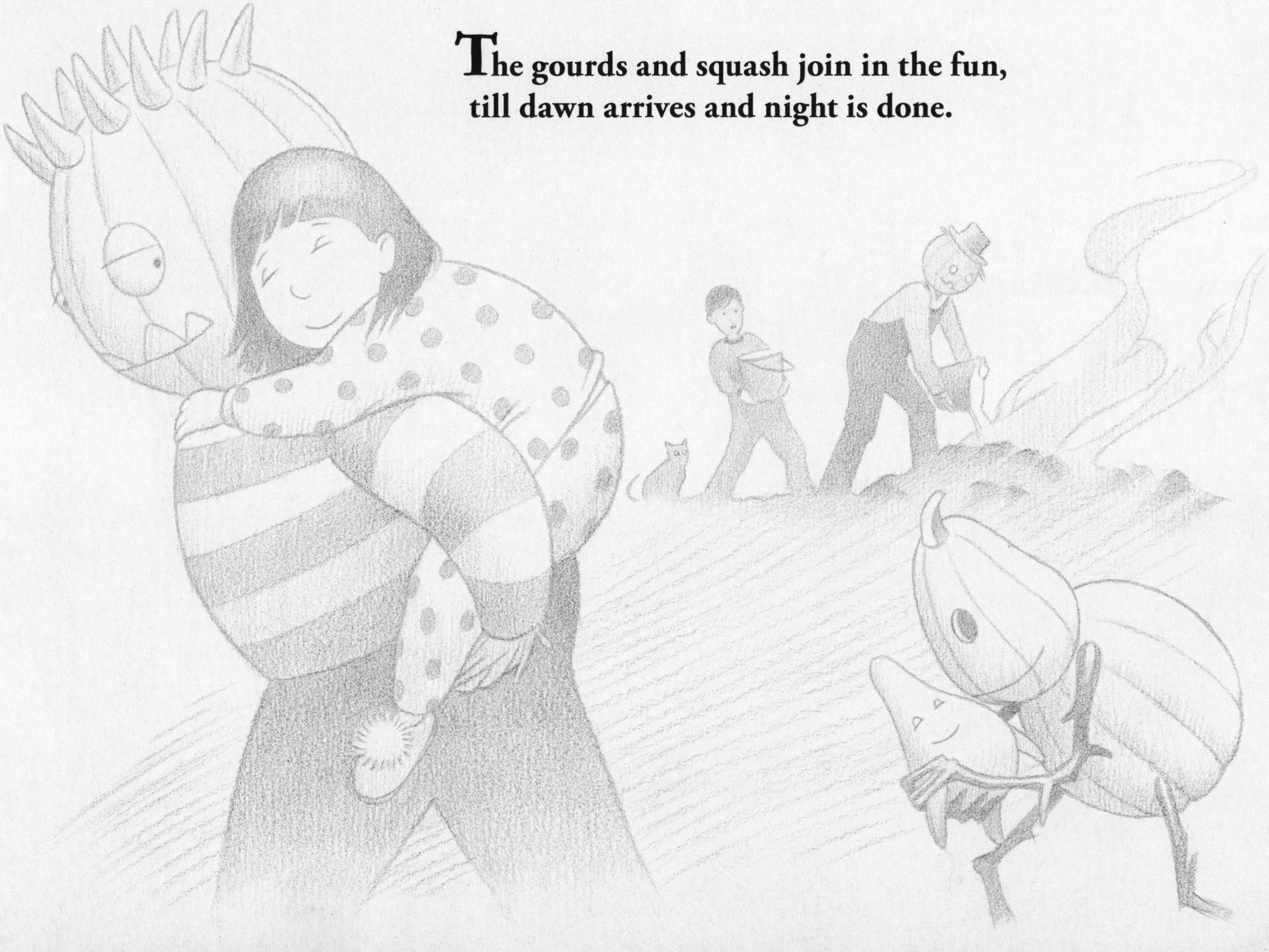

They sneak away without a trace.
By morning they are back in place.

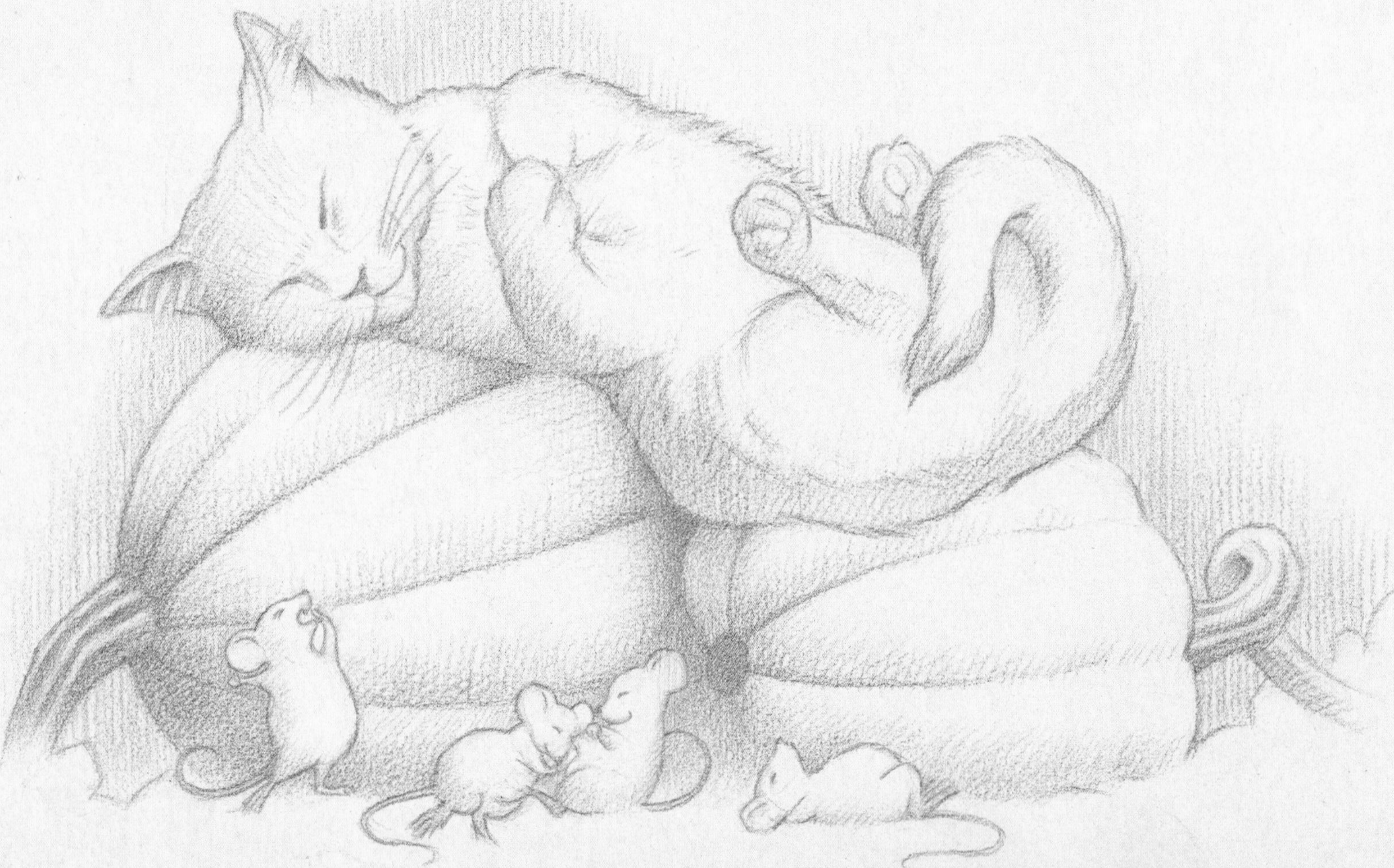

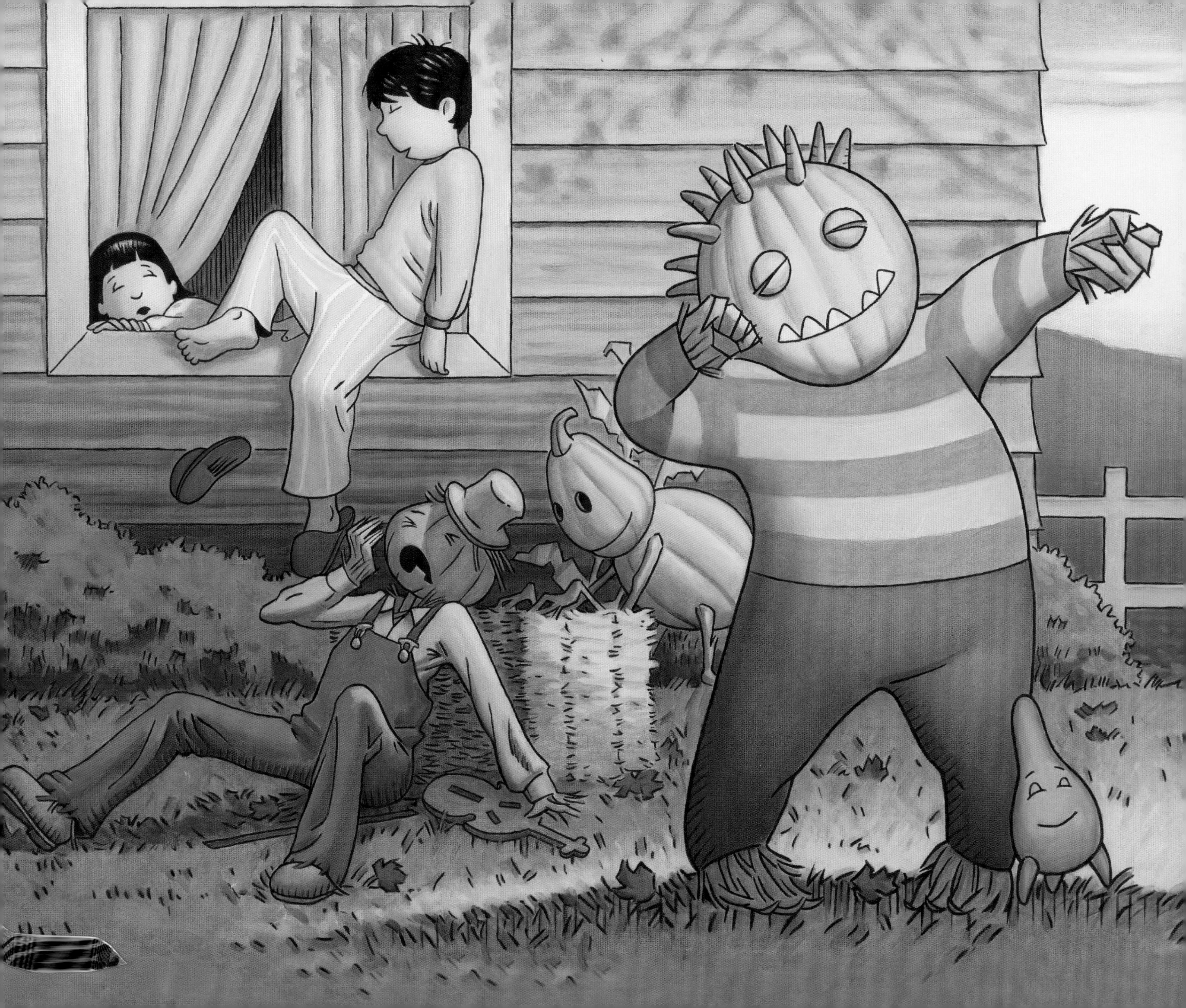

When the days grow cold and crisper
and the bleak winds sigh and whisper,

snowflakes tumble from the sky
and harvest folk must say goodbye.

Our friends are gone and so we wait
till spring when seeds will germinate.

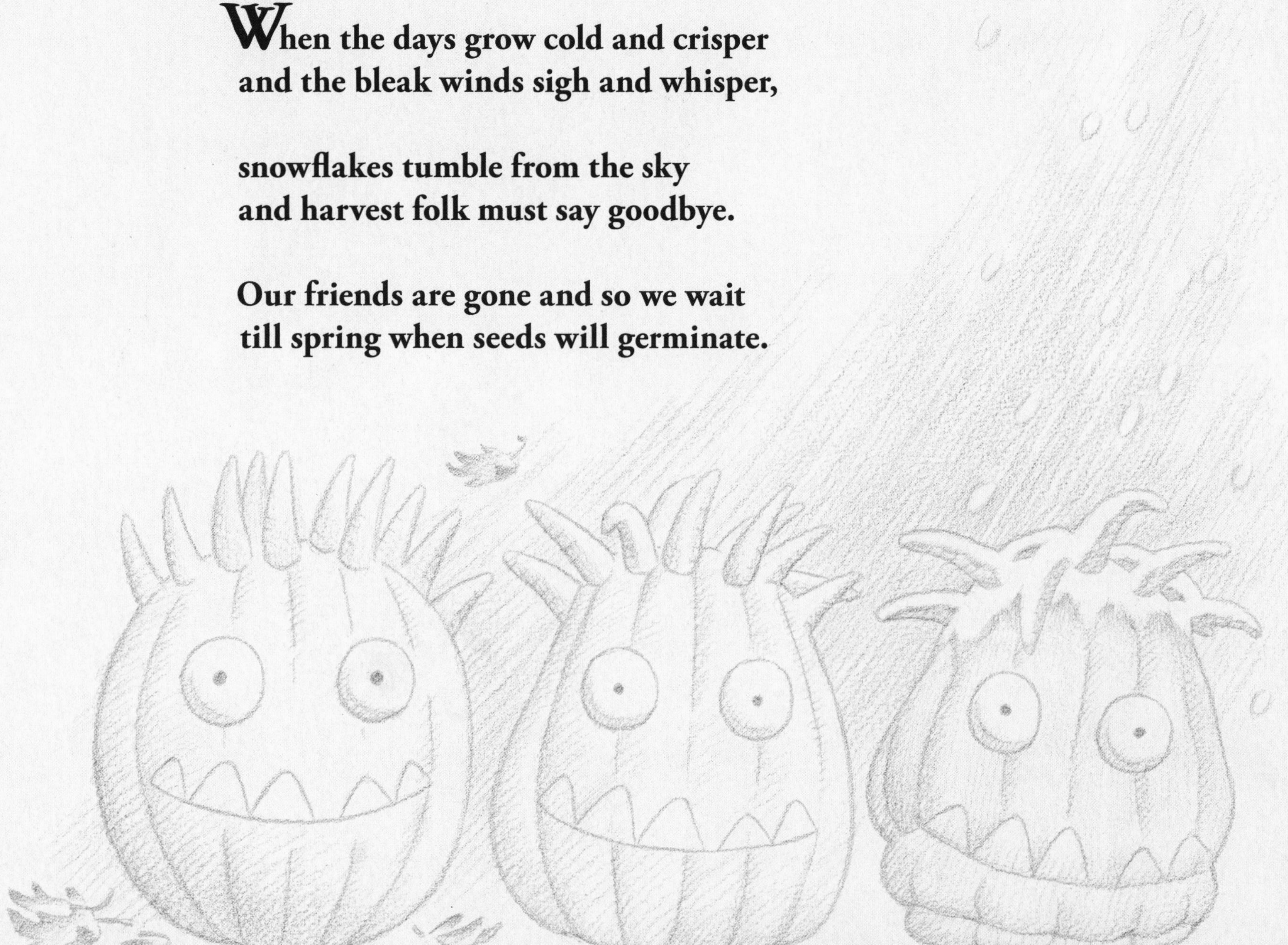

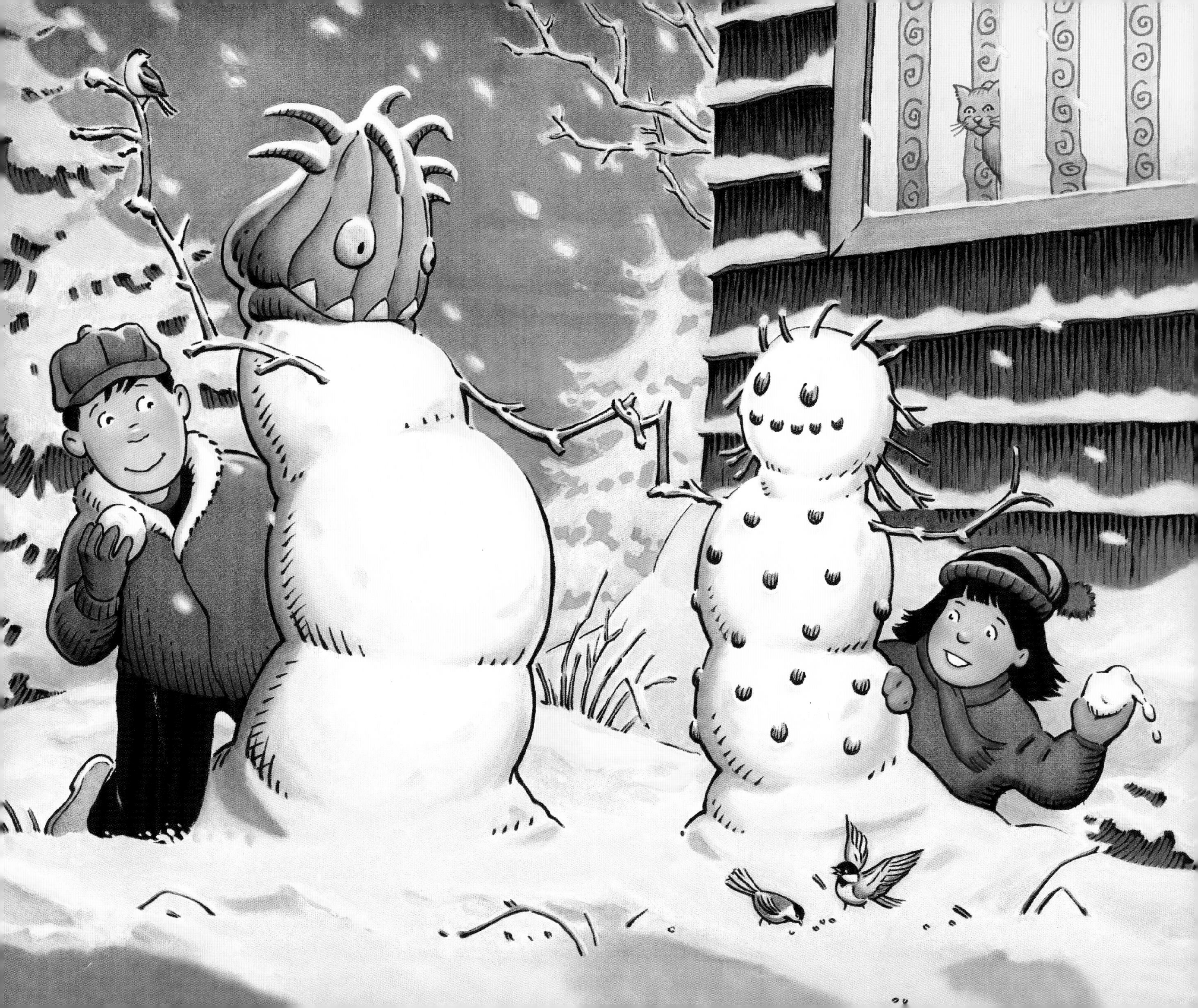

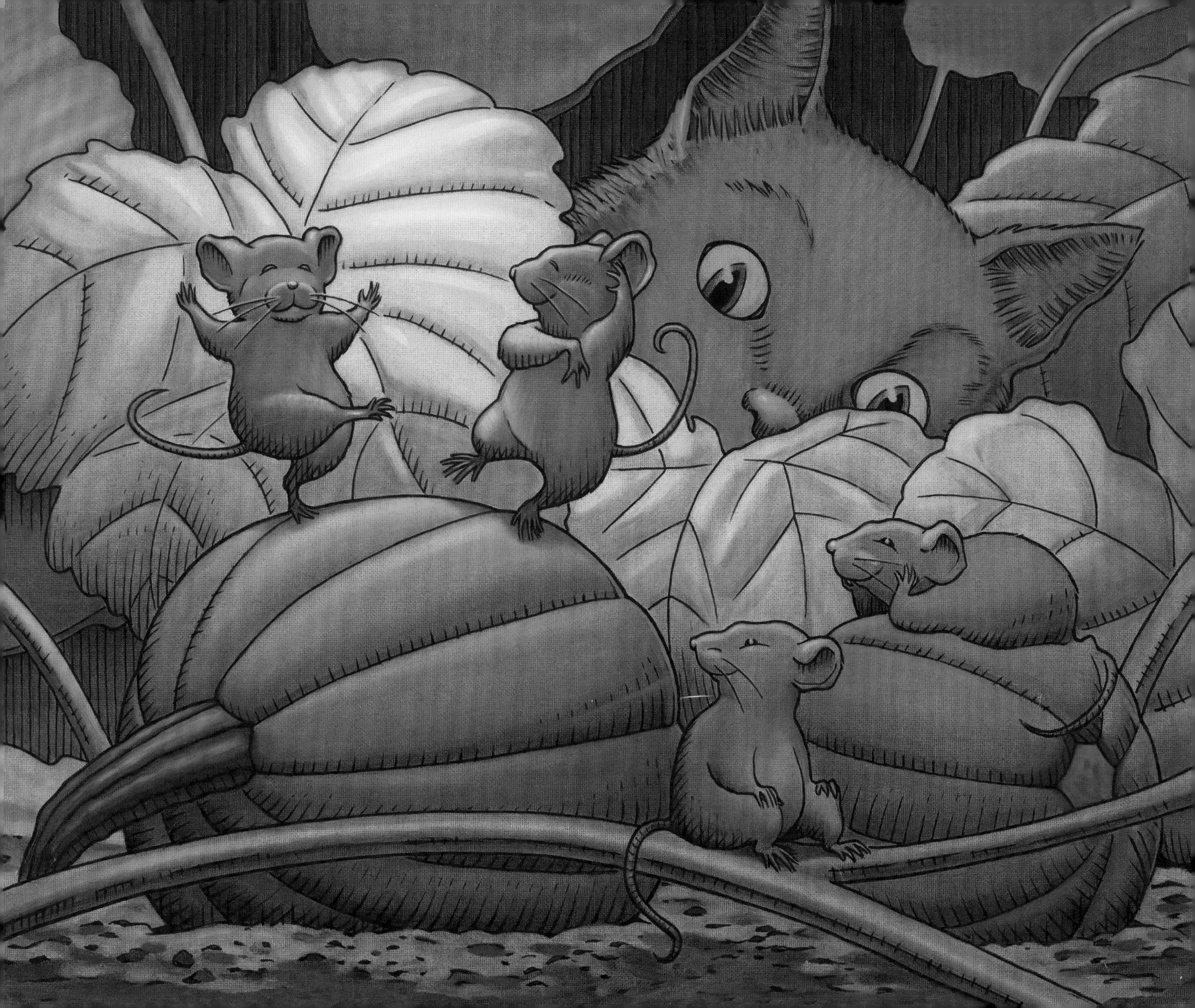

Then summer comes and plants grow tall
foretelling of our friends in fall.

And as the seasons come and go
the pumpkin people start to grow.

Awaiting nights beneath the moon
when pumpkins dance and play a tune.

Their secret's known to very few
but now it's also known… to you.

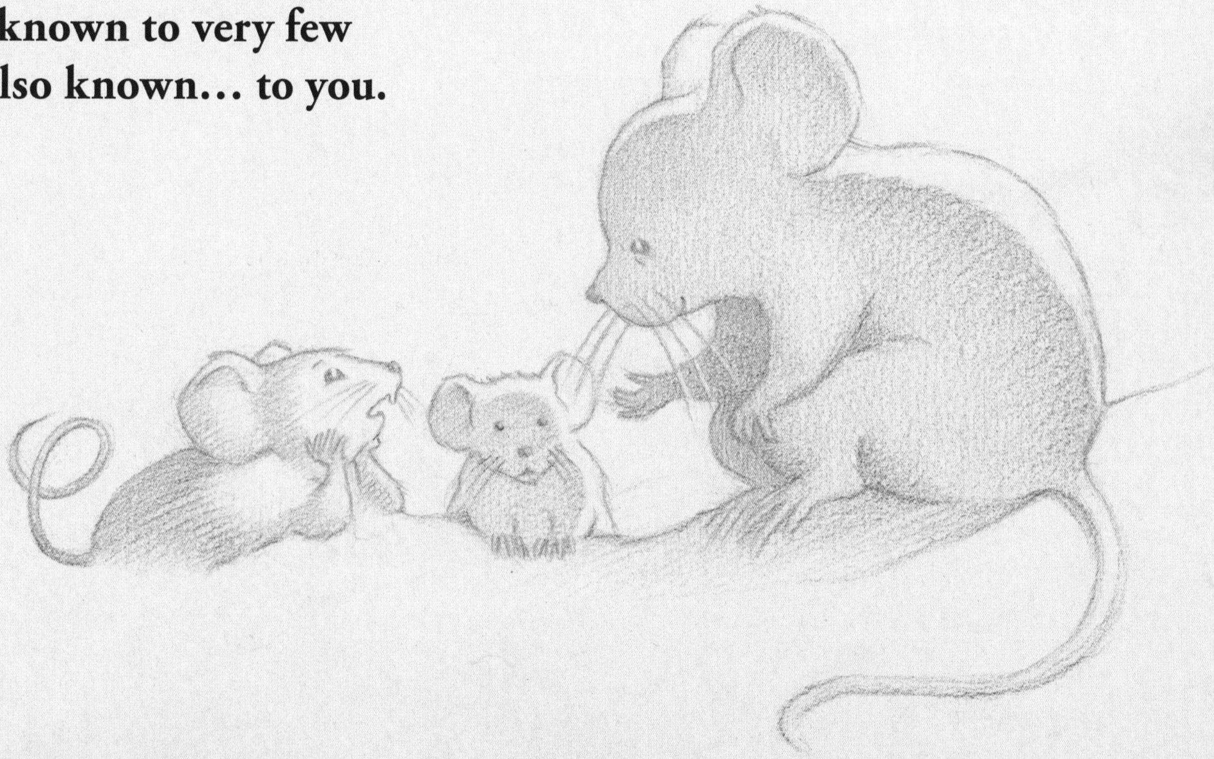

HOW TO MAKE YOUR OWN PUMPKIN PERSON

THINGS YOU WILL NEED
- about 11 cornstalks
- wide clear sticky tape
- scissors to cut tape
- hay, straw, or newspaper for stuffing
- old clothes
- pumpkin
- acrylic paints
- *Optional:* 1 × 3 inch strapping / wire / hand saw

HOW TO MAKE THE BODY

Arms
You will need 2 or 3 cornstalks, bundled in opposite directions. Wrap the tape around them tightly near the top and the bottom to make a bundle.

Body and Legs
You will need 2 bundles of 2 to 4 cornstalks, each taped at the top and bottom.

Body: To make the body, wrap tape tightly around both bundles at one end to create the neck and in the middle to create the waist.

Legs: Separate and bend the two bundles of cornstalks below the waist. Wrap the tape tightly around each leg near the ankles.

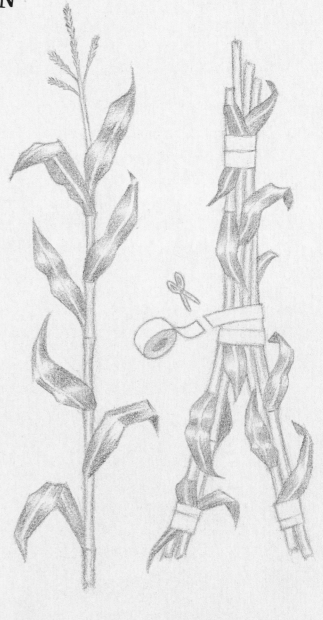

Finished Body

Now you are ready to attach the arms. Hold the arms across the body, about 12 to 15 centimeters (5 or 6 inches) from the top of the cornstalks. Tape the arms tightly to the body, wrapping the tape from the top of one shoulder to the bottom of the opposite shoulder. Go around and around about 4 times each way.

Bend the cornstalks to make shoulders, elbows, waist, and knees.

DRESSING YOUR PUMPKIN PERSON

Gently pull on the old clothes you have picked out for your pumpkin person. Some pumpkin people like to wear dresses, others like overalls or jeans. Some like bright colours and others like soft or dark colours. Anything goes when dressing your pumpkin person. After your pumpkin person is dressed, stuff the clothes firmly with hay, straw, or newspaper. Hot glue or pin the waistband and top together. (This helps to keep the stuffing from falling out.) Next cut a hole in the bottom of your pumpkin (big enough for the cornstalk neck to go into) and push the pumpkin down onto the neck.

HELPING YOUR PUMPKIN PERSON TO STAND

(Ask an adult to help you with this part.)

To make your pumpkin person stand up, use a piece of 1 × 3 strapping that is sharp at one end. Drive it into the ground where you want your pumpkin person to stand. Slide one leg of your pumpkin person over the strapping and slowly keep sliding them down until the strapping protrudes at the neck. Attach the cornstalk neck of the pumpkin person to the strapping with tape or wire and cut off any excess strapping. You can use a shorter piece of strapping driven into the ground to support the other leg.

ADDING A FACE TO YOUR PUMPKIN PERSON

The last step in making a pumpkin person is to paint a face on the head. You may wish to paint the face first before placing it on the neck, or take the head off your pumpkin person so it is easier to paint. Use acrylic paints so you can use water to clean your brushes and hands when you have finished painting.

Use your imagination to create an unusual head for your pumpkin person. You may want to cut some round holes (not too deep) at the top of the head and push the big end of a carrot into each hole. The carrots will wilt and look like hair. Small gourds can be used for noses, eyes, or ears. Create your pumpkin person with materials that are available to you. If you don't have cornstalks, use branches, dowelling or 1 × 2 or 1 × 4 lumber for the body and limbs. Have fun and let your imagination soar!

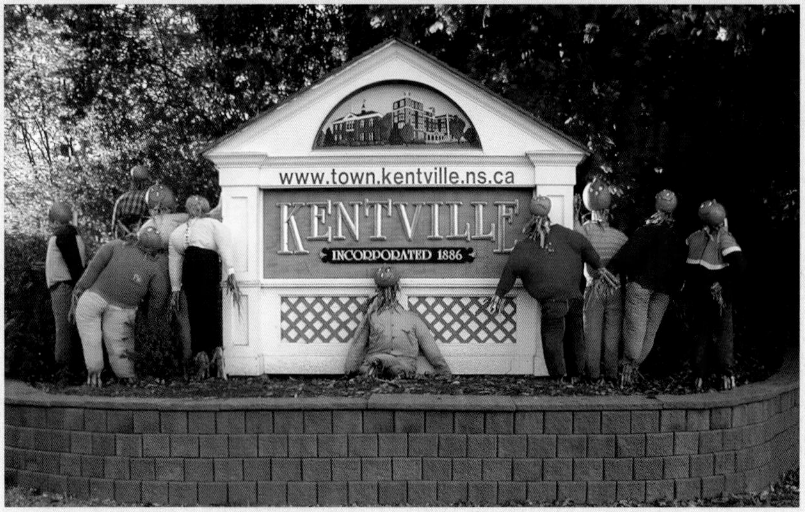
www.town.kentville.ns.ca
KENTVILLE
INCORPORATED 1886

THE KENTVILLE HARVEST FESTIVAL

In the spring of 1997 we moved to the beautiful Annapolis Valley in Nova Scotia, a vibrant community rich in cultural history, fertile farmland, and abundant apple orchards. Autumn brought the spectacular colours of fall, along with the arrival of many special visitors to the Town of Kentville. These unusual townsfolk had large orange heads, cornstalk bones, and lots of personality! We had discovered the annual gathering of the Pumpkin People, who help celebrate the Kentville Harvest Festival. When we saw hundreds of these fun figures cavorting throughout the town, we knew we had moved to our kind of place! We learned that each year brings a different theme for the Pumpkin People displays. We have seen them playing all kinds of sports, enacting scenes from famous fairy tales, and one of our favorite themes was when they appeared as spooky Halloween characters.

And as we saw the Pumpkin People reappear from year to year, we couldn't help but wonder what they did at night while the town slept. We thought other people might also be interested to know the answer. This question inspired us to create our book, *Pumpkin People.*

We would like to dedicate our book to the Town of Kentville (town.kentville.ns.ca) which welcomes a new family of Pumpkin People each year during their Harvest Festival in October. This festival highlights the area's agricultural industry and celebrates the harvest season from beginning to end. Thousands of visitors from all over the world make Kentville a destination point during their autumn tour of the province. Activities include hay wagon rides, crafts, art exhibits, community bands, buskers, competitions, and of course a lot of great local produce to eat.

We hope that you will have the opportunity to come and experience the Kentville Harvest Festival and to meet the friendly Pumpkin People. Who knows? Maybe they will come to life for *you*…

Sandra and Ron Lightburn

Nimbus Publishing Limited
PO Box 9166
Halifax, NS   B3K 5M8
(902) 455-4286   www.nimbus.ca

Printed and bound in Canada

Design: Co. & Co.
Author/illustrator photo: Eden's Garden Photography, Kentville, NS

Library and Archives Canada Cataloguing in Publication

    Lightburn, Sandra
    Pumpkin people / Sandra Lightburn ;
    Ron Lightburn, illustrator.
    ISBN 978-1-55109-681-0

1. Pumpkin—Juvenile fiction. 2. Harvest festivals—Nova Scotia—Kentville—Juvenile fiction. I. Lightburn, Ron II. Title.

PS8573.I415P84 2008   jC813'.54   C2008-904052-X

We acknowledge the financial support of the Government of Canada through the Book Publishing Industry Development Program (BPIDP) and the Canada Council, and of the Province of Nova Scotia through the Department of Tourism, Culture and Heritage for our publishing activities.

The Pumpkin People are a registered trademark of the Town of Kentville.

Photo on page 31 used with permission of the Town of Kentville.

The illustrations in this book were rendered using coloured pencils, acrylic paints and/or oil paints.

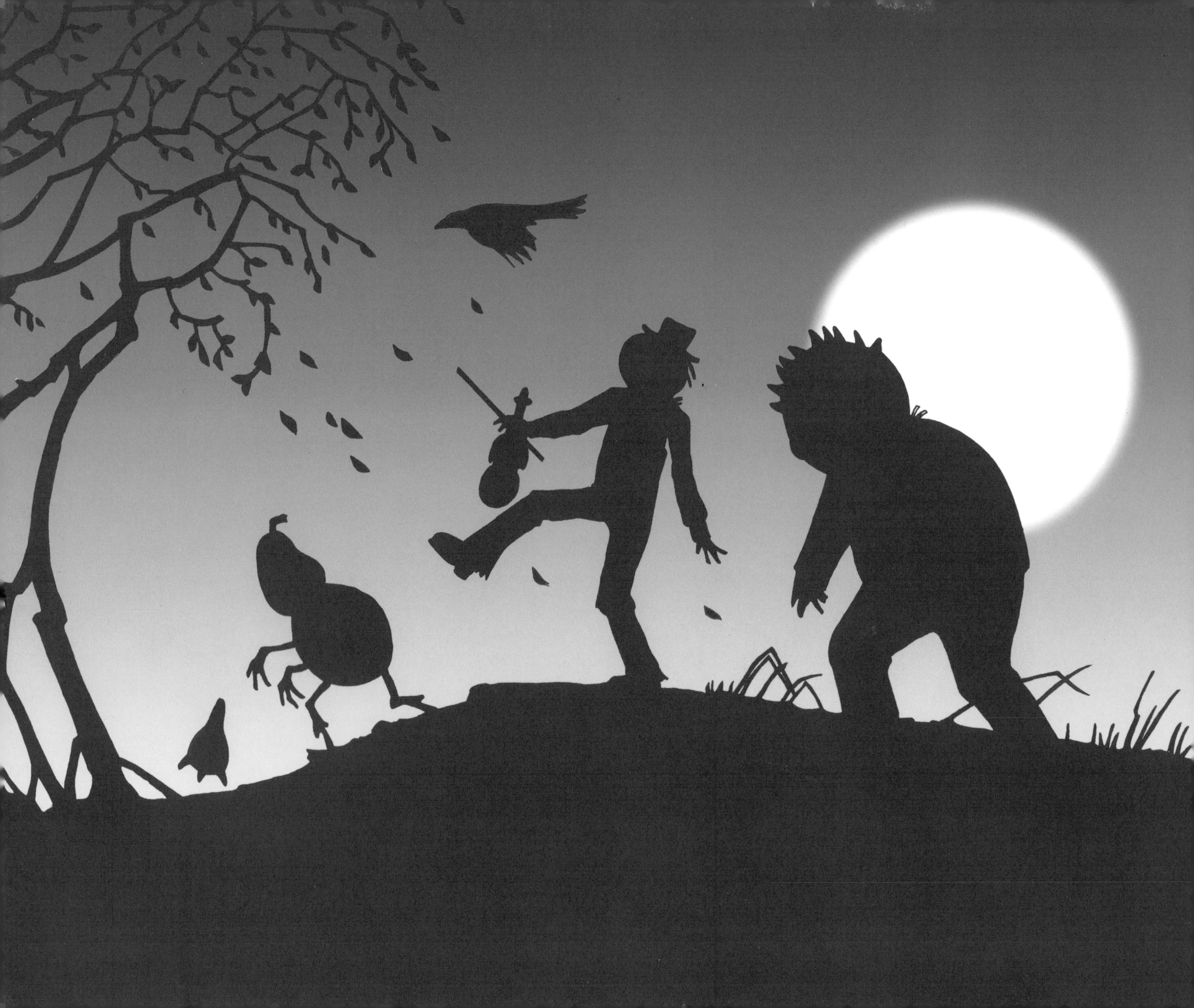